Love Don't Live Here Anymore...
It Just Visits Every Now & Then

Angela Weathered

"Love Don't Live Here Anymore ... It Just Visits Every Now and Then" by Angela Weathered. ISBN 1-58939-134-9 (softcover), 1-58939-135-7 (electronic).

Published 2002 by Virtualbookworm.com Publishing Inc., P.O. Box 9949, College Station, TX , 77842, US. © 2002 Angela Weathered. All rights reserved. No part of this publication may be reproduced, stored in a retrieval system, or transmitted in any form or by any means, electronic, mechanical, recording or otherwise, without the prior written permission of Angela Weathered.

Manufactured in the United States of America.

This book is dedicated to the memory of my grandmother, Katie M. Mays and my Home Economics Teacher, Marie DeRamus- two women that really played a major part in my life. I know that God is smiling down on the both of you!

Acknowledgments

I'd like to thank the following:

My husband, Kurt "Bull" for putting up with me those late nights while I was typing away on the computer.

My children- D'Ambra & Kurt Jr.- you two are truly a God send. You have made me very proud of you.

My mom- Barbara, thank you for giving me the gift of life

My sisters- Judy and Dianne- My "Older" sisters might I add, for not making your younger sister's life too miserable growing up. (smiling atcha! Wink, wink)

My nieces- Katrice, Brea and great-nieces Kierra and Julyah- be strong young ladies and you will make it far.

My nephews- Tyreto Jr., Stanley Jr., Terry Jr., Jamarcus & DeQuanyale- You are tomorrow's future- make us proud.

My mother-in-law, Francis- thanks you and God for giving me my special blessing "Bull".

My sister-in-laws, Tammy & Sherinaka- keep it real

My brother-in-laws, Old Man Stanley and Herman (Jay-Boogie)- I ain't mad atcha!

My sidekick, DeQuanta (Dee) at Turn Heads Hair Studio- may we continue to

"Turn Heads"!

My play-play little sister, Andrea- Keep your head up and keep singing those sweet songs of praise.

My good friends Lakethia & Brad- I wouldn't trade you two for all of the greens in Georgia!

My girls at Rivertown School of Beauty- Nicole (best friend-smiling atcha), Katrina (Shun), Kim, Kierra, Katrina (grandma), Brittany, Theresa, Vonnie, Feliciette, Noddia, Diana, Tiffany, Bernice, Annie, Jennifer, Amanda and my boy Paul-you hang in there boy!

Last, but certainly not least, my two other babies- my Rottweillers, Shaka Zulu and Neffretti- I love you all too!

Much love to all of you! Peace........

Angela AKA Nubiangodess

www.nubiangodess.com

Visit 1

"I'm so tired of this mess!"

Mama grabbed her head as she fell back onto the couch. The loud thump of her large frame, as it landed on the sofa, shook the framed picture of Black Jesus that was mounted on the wall behind it. With three good legs left on it, the sofa couldn't take much more of that kind of abuse. The brass lamp on the table next to the sofa wobbled like a pregnant woman in her last month of pregnancy, threatening to fall to the floor at any moment.

As usual, she was referring to the fact that her father was sick again and that we lived too far away from him to just pick up and drive to see about him. Besides, we didn't have a car to drive even if we did want to go. It hurt mama very much knowing that she couldn't do anything to help Granny. We lived over a thousand miles away from them. Being in Columbus was just too depressing for her. That's why she left in the first place.

Mama and daddy were having serious marital problems. They'd been having them for a while, and I guess she finally got tired of his ass and decided that she could do bad all by herself. If she had to struggle due to his not contributing, be it financially or physically, she'd rather struggle on her own. It's not like daddy was all that, so I don't know how he was getting all of those women to begin with. First of all, he was chubby, going bald, half of his teeth were missing, and he still wore polyester. I don't think that would qualify him to be 'God's gift to women'.

They had their share of problems like any other married couple, but daddy didn't seem like he wanted to change. He would leave home as soon as he got up in the morning and wouldn't return until early in the morning, if at all. Frankly, I would have put him out a long time ago. I'm sure she knew that something was going on

"James, I want to talk to you!"

"I don't have time right now, Maxine, I have to get to the pool hall."

"But I really need to talk to you. It's important."

"Is it so important that it can't wait until I get back home?"

"And when will that be? Five, six in the morning? Tomorrow? Just tell me, James!"

"Listen woman! Don't go starting that shit with me again, you hear, cause I don't have time for it!"

"Just like you don't have time for me and them kids of yours huh. You run around here like you're somebody with all these different women. It's a shame before God that you can take care of them, and you don't even care if your own children have food on the table."

"Now there you go accusing me of that shit again. How many times do I have to tell you that I ain't been messing with nobody? I'm getting tired of you accusing me of it too!"

"What are these James?" Mama said, reaching into her apron pocket to retrieve two rubbers.

He stood there looking dumb-founded.

"Tell me James, what were these doing in your wallet? I had my tubes tied four years ago, so I know you aren't using them so I won't get knocked up!"

"I don't have to explain shit to you! What the hell are you doing going through my wallet anyway?"

Mama didn't answer. She'd finally gotten her answer from him. She had the evidence that she needed to finally realize that he was no good for her. It had been a long, hard journey up until this point, and she had been in denial for a long time. So many nights I laid awake listening to mama and daddy arguing back and forth.

Love Don't Live Here Anymore

I use hear stuff being thrown against the walls. Daddy would yell at mama, and slap her around. She'd start screaming at the top of her lungs, telling him to leave. A few minutes later, daddy would come stomping out of the room, slamming the door behind him. Mama would lay in her bed and cry all night long. She let him put her through so much unnecessary pain.

Daddy was definitely a smooth talker. He'd explain away every accusation she made. It must have been her love for him that made her forgive him each time, because she definitely wasn't using her common sense to guide her. I use to hear mama say "My babies ain't growing up without they daddy. We gone be a family if it kills me!" As much as I wanted to tell her that it just might, I couldn't bring myself to do it.

One night when daddy got home from work, she had dinner waiting on the table. All of the candles were lit, and mama had on a new dress. She really looked nice. You think daddy noticed? He told her that he wasn't hungry and that he was changing clothes and leaving. The fellas were having a get together. These days, the fellas were his top priority. Mama was devastated. He got dressed and left without even touching his food.

We couldn't understand why mama wouldn't leave daddy. It wasn't that much love in the world. My oldest sister use to always tell her how she felt.

"Mama, why don't you just leave his sorry behind. You can do better than him anyway!" She didn't care. We were all tired of the way daddy was treating her, but she was the only one strong enough to speak up about how she felt. Mama would always defend daddy though.

"He's just going through something right now. He'll come out of it," she said. Maybe she actually thought that he would get tired of doing her wrong.

One night she came home from work early only to find him and her best friend, Roxanne, making out in their bed. The one that they'd shared for more than twenty years. I guess that's what she got for helping a 'friend' in need. Mama had given her a place to stay, fed her, and half the time clothed her too. She didn't want for anything. Needless to say, mama and Roxanne weren't best friends very much longer.

When the lights came on, daddy jumped straight up out of the bed. All he could do was stand there looking dumb-founded, holding his still-erect penis. He jumped so quickly, the momentum threw Roxanne to the floor. She quickly grabbed for the sheets, but couldn't find any.

Mama blinked her eyes several times as if the awful sight would go away, but it didn't. It was no surprise to her that daddy was cheating, but she was really hurt that her best friend, for more than twenty years, could do something so terrible to her. Without warning, mama's legs gave way, and she dropped to the floor.

I think the thing with Roxanne was the straw that finally broke the camel's back. She'd finally given up on the thought that daddy would change his ways. She was fighting a useless battle. "You can't love someone that doesn't want to be loved," she said, finally convincing herself.

Having to leave my grandparents was one of the most difficult things she had to do. She knew they were getting old and that my grandfather had been sick a long time. She wasn't doing him any good by staying in Columbus because she was depressed all of the time. Granddaddy had basically given up his will to live, so he didn't care what mama did. My grandmother, on the other hand, gave her blessings, and we were on our way north.

After finally deciding that things weren't going to get any better, mama decided to move. She called one of her friends in Michigan and asked him to help her find a place to stay when we arrived. It wasn't going to be easy; but neither was living with daddy. We packed our bags and took the next Greyhound Bus to Michigan.

When we got there, mama's friend welcomed us with open arms, but after five months of freeloading, we moved into our own apartment. Mama met a new man, and he took care of us. Leroy was fifteen years her senior, and he was married. He had kids that were mama's age, but that didn't seem to matter to her. I guess she figured that since somebody took her man, she was going to get her another one, regardless of whether they had someone or not. Leroy was just about bald on the top of his head, but he had a complete Afro on the sides and in the back. He had a serious horseshoe look going on. He was six-two and weighed about two-thirty. In his younger days, I suppose, he could have been nice looking.

The fact that he had a wife and seven children didn't seem to bother mama or Leroy. They were bold with their affair. He'd take us on family outings and stuff, or he'd come over to our house after work and stay until one or two o'clock in the morning like he didn't have a care in the world. Mama and him would be all locked up in her room from the time he got there, until the time he left. I was always curious as to what was going on behind those closed doors.

One night my friend, Ebony, called and asked me to come over. Leroy was getting ready to leave, so I ran downstairs to ask him if he could give me a ride.

"Mr. Leroy!" I yelled, looking up at him. "Will you give me a ride to my friend, Ebony's house? I want to spend the night with her".

"Did you ask yo mama?" he said.

"Yes Sir, and she told me to come down here and ask you."

"Well go tell her that I said yes, and come on," he yelled.

I ran as fast as I could. I couldn't wait to see Ebony.

I was about to climb into the back seat of the van as I always did, but Mr. Leroy told me to come up front with him. Although I knew it wasn't safe for me to ride up front, I dare not question a grownup. That was a big no-no! I knew that mama would beat my butt if I had.

Mr. Leroy pulled out of our apartment complex, but he didn't take me to Ebony's house, instead, he took me over to his friend's house. It was very dark on the inside, so I knew there wasn't anyone there. I was so scared.

"Mr. Leroy, this ain't Ebony's house!" I said, scared that he was going to backhand me for talking back.

"I know that Shaneeka!" he snapped.

"Ebony's mama told me to bring you over here and she was going to pick you up later" he said, lying the whole time.

We got out of the van and walked inside. Apparently who ever lived there knew Mr. Leroy very well because he had keys to their house. When we entered, the house was very dark. There was a small crack in the blinds that let in a little light from the streetlights outside, but that was all there was.

He didn't turn on any lights inside. He seemed to know the house pretty well, because he found his way around in the dark. He reached inside a closet and pulled out a blanket and a pillow.

"What's that for, Mr. Leroy?" I asked growing more scared by the second.

"Just take this and lay down over there on the floor."

I did as I was told.

He looked at me with his cold, gray eyes and said, "What's that?" touching me where my breasts would later be. My heart began to pound so hard, I thought for sure that he could hear it.

When I tried to get up and run, he grabbed me around my waist and pulled me close to him. I could feel something hard in his pants poking me as he rubbed his body against mine. His breathing grew more rapid by the second. I could smell his breath as he kissed me on my neck. I can still smell his scent even to this day.

He began to unzip his pants, which scared me even more. By this time, he'd put his hand over my mouth so that I couldn't scream. My eyes were wide open with fear. I'd never seen anything like that before in my life. His penis was sticking out of his pants. It seemed to grow before my eyes. He made me touch it. I was petrified. I got nauseous.

He pulled my shorts down and began rubbing me between my legs. I didn't know what he was doing, but I knew it wasn't right. He pulled me on top of him and forced his tongue into my mouth. I threw up everything that I'd eaten that day, all over the blanket. That made Mr. Leroy mad. He reached back and slapped me so hard, I thought I saw stars. I began to cry, but no one could hear me.

"Get over here!" he yelled, pulling me by my hair.

Just as he grabbed me by the back of my head, there was a knock at the door. He quickly put his hand over my mouth and whispered into my ear "If you make a sound, I will kill you!" I was so scared that I peed on myself. There was another knock. He got up and walked over to the blind and peeked out. Whoever it was at the door left. I guess it took him too long to answer.

When he came back over to me, he saw that I had peed on myself. He shook his head in disgust, and went in the bathroom and got a wash cloth and threw it at me like I was some kind of animal or something.

"Here, take this and clean yourself up!" He said and walked out of the room.

After I was finished, I went back into the living room. By this time, he was fully dressed.

"If you tell anyone what happened here today, I will kill your whole family, do you hear me!" Mr. Leroy shouted.

I knew that he meant every word he said. I shook my head and said "Yes Sir!" while wiping the tears from my eyes.

He dropped me off at Ebony's house and went on his merry way as though nothing had just happened. I watched out of the window as he slowly backed out of the driveway. Our eyes made contact one last time as he mouthed the threats to me once more.

"Remember what I told you!" and pulled away.

What had I done to make him touch me the way he did? That pervert! Was that what was happening when mama's door was closed? I didn't even want to play any more. Ebony and me went up stairs and talked until be both fell asleep. I didn't dare tell her about what had just happened to me. I didn't want Mr. Leroy to kill my mama or my sisters. My lips were sealed forever!

When I got home, mama was waiting on me at the front door.

"How was your time at Ebony's house, Shaneeka?"

"Mama, can we talk about something else? I asked. She must not have really been interested anyway, because she didn't bother to ask why I didn't want to talk about my visit.

"Mama, can you find you a new boyfriend?" I asked, knowing she wasn't trying to hear a word I was saying.

"Leroy is a good man! I deserve to be happy and ain't you or nobody else gone take that from me, you hear me!" she shouted.

I couldn't believe what I was hearing. That was the day I lost total respect for my mother.

Before Mr. Leroy came into mama's life, we had a good relationship. Now, her only concern was pleasing him. I started to rebel. I wanted to get attention, and the only way I could do that was to act up. It was negative attention, but I guess that was better than nothing. I hated Mr. Leroy for taking mama away from me. He had his own family. He had his own wife. Why did he have to come and take my mama from me?

Whenever he came around, I'd roll my eyes at him. He'd speak, but I wouldn't speak back. He knew what he'd done to me was wrong. I knew it. But yet, he thought everything was going to be the same. It made me sick to my stomach every time I saw him. I often wondered how many other little girls he'd touched the way he touched me. How many others he'd threatened to kill if they told his dirty little secrets..

I started staying away from home as much as possible. I'd get up in the morning, get dressed and leave. I'd come home just in time to go to bed. Mama didn't care what I did as long as I stayed out of her and Leroy's way. I often stayed with my best friend, Angelina, until her mother gave me that I-don't-mind-you-coming-over-here-but-it's-time-for-you-to-go-home-now-look! I understood because she had ten kids of her own to raise. She didn't need me around twenty four-seven.

Angelina and I were walking around the apartment complex when we noticed a moving truck. We immediately stopped to see what was going on, when out of nowhere, came the finest thing you ever wanted to see! He was about five nine, two hundred pounds, and was sporting sandy colored dreadlocks. His skin was the color of cappuccino with just a kiss of cream added. He wasn't wearing a shirt, so you could see his six pack very clearly. It was intoxicating. I didn't realize that I was staring so hard until Angelina poked me in my shoulder with her finger.

"Hello, I'm Marcus!" he said in his smooth voice. I could have melted, but I controlled myself. We both introduced ourselves.

Marcus had just moved to Saginaw from Jacksonville, Florida. His mother was a nurse and had just accepted a promotion, which brought them to Michigan. Lucky for me! He was an only child, so he spent much of his time alone. This was perfect because all I had was time on my hands. As the days went on, we began to spend more and more time together. We'd sit on his porch for hours, talking about all the things we wanted to accomplish in life. Marcus wanted to be a doctor. I told him that I'd always wanted to be a lawyer specializing in Family Law.

I guess Angelina begin to feel like a third wheel, so she made up some lame excuse as to why she had to leave. Marcus and I sat on the corner and talked for what seemed like hours. He shared with me how his parents had never gotten married, but that they'd lived together his whole life. His mom got a promotion, but she had to relocate to another state. His dad, simply, wasn't willing to leave his job. That's the reason they went their separate ways. Atleast they still loved each other. Unlike my parent's situation, it wasn't because of another woman. Maybe one day they will reach some kind of agreement that would allow them to reunite and still keep their jobs.

I'd only known Marcus for about twenty-five minutes, yet it seemed like I'd known him a lifetime. I began to pour out my soul to him. I just needed someone to talk to. My life was so screwed up it wasn't funny. He was willing to listen to me. He didn't judge me; he just listened to what I had to say. Something I felt my mom should have done. Instead, she chose her man.

It didn't take a genius to tell that something was wrong with me. Marcus read me easily.

"What's wrong Shaneeka? You look so sad!" he said in a real concerned voice.

I tried to deny that there was anything wrong, but he saw right through me. It was kind of scary that he could read me so easily. I didn't tell him everything that happened. I just told him that I was going through some things at home, and I just needed someone to listen to me and be there for me. Someone to be concerned about how I was feeling.

"You don't have to go into details, Shaneeka. Anytime you need me, I'll be there for you. You can count on that!" he said, and gave me a huge bear hug.

He continued, "Besides, that's what friends are for."

That was something I really needed to hear. Marcus came into my life just in the nick of time.

It started getting dark outside, so he walked me home. As we reached my front door, he pulled me close to him, and before I knew it, he'd planted a big juicy kiss on my lips. It felt so good! Having his arms around me didn't make me feel dirty like I did when Mr. Leroy touched me. This felt right. Just as I was about to kiss him back, the porch light came on. Mama started yelling for me to get my "fass ass" in the house. I was embarrassed, but I wasn't crazy. I knew that she meant what she said, so I gave him another quick peck, and ran into the house.

Mama gave me an ear full. She called me everything but a child of God! She forbid me to ever see Marcus again.

"You gone end up knocked up messing round wit these lil nappy headed boys, and I ain't gon take care of no babies!" she yelled.

Yeah right! I went to my room and closed the door.

Marcus and me walked home from school together everyday. He even carried my books like a perfect little gentleman. Sometimes we would take the long way home just so we could talk.

"One day Shaneeka, you gone be my wife," Marcus said.

He just came right out of the blue and said that. I looked at him, all embarrassed. I didn't know what to say. He caught me totally off guard. He was so sure of himself. I think that's what I liked most about him. Whenever he set his mind on doing something, he did just that. He wasn't going to get any arguments from me.

One day Marcus' mom was working late, so he invited me over to play his video game. This was our favorite pass-time. He went into the kitchen to get us a bite to eat. When he returned to the living room, he sat the tray of food down onto the table and came over to me. He got down on one knee and reached for my hand. He slid a piece of aluminum foil, rolled to resemble a wedding band, onto my finger and asked me to be his wife.

"Marcus, what's this for?" I asked him looking down at my finger.

"We can't get engaged without a ring, now can we?" he asked

"We're only fourteen years old, we can't get married," I said.

"I'm not asking you to run off and marry me tomorrow, unless you want to, but I do want you as my wife some day" he said, not skipping a beat.
"Hold on to this ring. One day I will be able to give you a real one," he said as he kissed me on my cheek.

It was getting late, so Marcus walked me home. I was on cloud nine. I was determined that nothing was going to steal my joy that night; not even seeing Mr. Leroy's van parked outside of our apartment.

I ran up to my room and closed my door. I wanted to have some quiet time to myself. Time to think about my future with Marcus. I was so wrapped up in my daydreams, that I almost used the bathroom on myself. I ran to the bathroom quickly. On my way out, I saw mama's bedroom door opening. Before I could react, my eyes met up with those cold gray eyes of Mr. Leroy's. He was standing there re-adjusting his pants. He looked down at me with this big smirk on his face. I quickly slammed the door.

The next morning, I was the only one at home. Mama was only God knows where, and my sisters were outside playing with our neighbors. I decided that it was time for Mr. Leroy's wife to know just what her husband was up to. I picked up the telephone and dialed his number. Some little kid answered.

"May I speak to your mom?" I asked.

"Mama, telephone!" the little girl shouted. Shortly afterwards, a woman's voice spoke into the telephone receiver.

"Hello!" she said, speaking just above a whisper. Her voice sounding too innocent to be treated the way that her husband so carelessly treated her.

"Is this Leroy's wife?"

"Yes, who is this?" she asked, sounding very puzzled.

"Listen, your husband is at my mama's house every night. And frankly, I'm tired of it. You need to keep him at home," I said and hung the telephone up.

I had it all figured out, but what I wasn't expecting her to do is *69 me. The phone rang only seconds after I hung up. I answered it, not knowing that it was Mrs. Leroy on the other end. She didn't even give me time to say hello. She started right in on me.

"Who is this?" she said.

"Who I am is not important. All you need to know is keep your husband away from my mama, or you're gonna wish you had." I hung up on her once again, feeling as though I'd accomplished something. This time, she didn't call back.

That night, when Mr. Leroy came over, I heard him and mama arguing. I knew I was going to be in trouble, but I didn't care. That served him right. Mama stumped out of her room and came and knocked on my door.

"Shaneeka, you get yo lil ass out here right now, you hear me!" she shouted.

I knew exactly what she wanted and why she was calling me. I stuck my chest out like I was somebody, and opened my door. Mr. Leroy was standing behind mama like the coward that he was.

"Did you call Leroy's house Shaneeka?" she asked, already knowing the answer to the question.

"No ma'am," I answered, lying through my teeth.

"Shaneeka, I'm not going to ask you again. Did you call Leroy's house telling his wife my business?"

"Yes ma'am," I answered, knowing I couldn't lie any longer. And then I got bold.

"Yeah, I called his wife. Why he gotta be over here all the time anyway? He needs to be at home with his wife and his own kids instead of over here messing our family up. Our lives were fine before he came into the picture. Now that he's here, he's all you seem to care about. I hate him, but I hate you even more!"

I turned to face mama.

"How could you do this to us mama? That's probably why daddy treated you the way that he did. I hate you and that freak of a boyfriend you have!" I shouted and ran out of the house.

Angela Weathered

There was no taking back the words that I'd spoken. I meant every one of them. I didn't know where I was going to go when I ran out of the house. I just knew that I couldn't stay around there anymore. I ran to the corner pay phone and called Ebony's mom collect. I asked her if she would come and get me, and she did.

When I got to their house, I wasn't asked a lot of questions because everyone could see that I was really upset. Ebony's mom held me close to her and comforted me; something my own mother should have been doing. I stayed for a week. On Friday when I got back from school, mama was waiting on me to take me home. On the way home, mama tried her best to talk to me. There was nothing she had to say that I wanted to hear. I knew where her priorities were; they weren't with me. I was just a stumbling block in her way. For the next several weeks, we barely said two words to one another.

Visit 2

The telephone rang about two o'clock in the morning. You knew it was bad news, because nobody calls your house that late at night unless someone has died, or is about dead. It was granny again. She called to tell us that my grandfather had another stroke (this was about the third one), and that his condition was getting worse every day. The doctors had given him less than six months to live. I knew exactly what that meant. Columbus, Georgia, here we come.

The next morning, mama called the welfare office to see if we could get some help paying for our move. Ms. Jackson, mama's caseworker, told her that they could send us on the bus. There we were, mama and her three daughters, about to pick up and move from the only place I'd ever known as home, to some foreign place so many miles away.

We arrived in Columbus in the summer of 1983. I thought my world had ended. I left all of my friends, along with the boy I was head over heels in love with, back in Saginaw, Michigan. I didn't want any new friends. I didn't want a new lifestyle. I didn't want anything, except to stay right where I was.

We went from living in a three-bedroom townhouse, to a one-bedroom hole-in-the-wall apartment. I tried not to complain because I knew that mama was doing the best she could considering our circumstances. We lived too far away from our school, so mama sent my sister and me to live at my grandparent's house.

Even though I didn't want to be there at first, I must admit it was kind of cool staying with my grandparents.

I had a lot more freedom living with them than I would've had living with my mama.

My grandparents went to bed early, so I would sneak out of the house late at night and go to the park across the street. There was a group of teenagers that hung out there. We'd sit around talking about stuff that we know we didn't have any business talking about. Sometimes the girls would tell stories about how many guys they'd slept with. One of the girls talked about her lesbian affairs. So as you can see, some of the conversations got kind of deep.

While everyone else had something to tell, I didn't, so I'd make stuff up. If I had told them that I was still a virgin, I would've been the laughing stock of the day, so naturally I lied. It wasn't hard for me to fantasize about being with Marcus, so that's what I did. I told them the things that I hoped Marcus would, some day, do to me.

I was the first one to leave every morning. I didn't want granny to tell mama about my sneaking out, because I would have to go back and stay with her. That wasn't about to happen.

Granny caught me coming in one morning about five-thirty.

"Where yo lil behind been girl?" she asked.

I couldn't tell her that I was outside with a bunch of boys. She'd give me the fifth degree then.

"I couldn't sleep, so I got up early and got ready for school. I was trying to do a little straightening up before I went to school, so I took the trash out." I hated lying, especially to my grandmother of all people. Everyone else, I could care less about. Granny was special, and she didn't deserve to be lied to. Being the kind person that she was, God rest her soul, she believed me.

If I got out of that lie, I promised myself, I would never lie to her again, I thought silently to myself. It looked as though she bought it.

"All right then, but you be careful cause there are some fools out there, and we don't want no trouble, you hear me?" she said. I shook my head and proceeded to my bedroom.

Angela Weathered

Visit 3

Granny was always talking about how good The Lord is. How He makes a way out of no way. I had a hard time believing it, because everything in my life had gone wrong. Things had been that way for the last couple years. I decided to go to church and give God a try. What did I have to lose? I got up early Sunday morning so I could get dressed. I slid into a mustard-colored, hip-hugging wrap skirt, a black knit turtleneck sweater, and my black leather, high-heeled boots. I had on just a hint of makeup; au natural is always best. I'd gone by Nubian Creations the day before and my girl, Erica, really hooked a sistah up. I knew I was looking good!

When I walked into the sanctuary, all eyes were on me. I knew that if I walked in late, everyone would turn around to see who was coming in. Don't hate me because I'm beautiful! I picked a sit closer to the rear of the church. That way, if the service got boring, or if they started asking for too much money, I could easily tip toe out the door. One thing that I learned about church people was that they believe in passing the offering plate around several times and staying in church all day on Sundays.

The minister was already up. He was preaching about how people need to get saved and give their lives to God. All I could think about was how long this man had been talking. Preachers are some long-winded people. The bench I was sitting on was hurting my butt, and, on top of that, the woman sitting behind me had the nerve to jump up and start screaming something right in my ear. Before I could react, she'd taken off running down the isle. I was scared as all get up. I couldn't help but to wonder what I'd gotten myself into.

Another lady on the other side of the church started speaking in tongues. The people never acted like that at the other church I went to. I could see why people called them Holy-rollers! The musician was about seventeen. He was up there playing that song by Rob Base called "It takes two". All the young people around me knew what he was playing, because as soon as he started, they all looked at him. Those old people didn't have a clue. They shouted until they got tired, sat down, and got back up and started all over again.

As I looked around the church again, I noticed that the drummer was starring at me. I turned my head hoping that he would stop, but he didn't. I just ignored him. He was very persistent, though. After the service was over, we left the church and went out to our car.

Mama parked away from the church, because she didn't want to draw any attention our 'vehicle'. You see, we had what you would call a hoopty for a car. Mama named it Betsy. Daddy bought it from a junk dealer so we'd have some transportation. He took a door from another car he had and put it on this one. He could have at least painted it the same color as our car. He tied a string around the passenger seat in the front to keep that door on. The back seat looked like an old couch, and the floor was so corroded, you could see the street through the holes in it. So you see, this car was the last one I wanted someone to see me getting into.

Just as I sat down something told me to look up, so I did. There he was again. The "drummer boy" was coming out of the church. He was walking backwards to keep me in his sight. I guess he thought that I was going to vanish into thin air or something. I thought it was rather funny until I realized he was walking in my direction. He wasn't very handsome at all, but I wasn't going to marry him tomorrow or anything. He introduced himself as Eric Johnson.

He was a tall, about six-one, very dark skinned, and had almost rose colored pink lips. Boy that was some combination. He was probably a hundred and fifty pounds soaking wet, yet there was something about him. I got a certain vibe from him when he got closer to me. I can't really describe it, but something in my heart was telling me to be gentle with him; don't bite his head off. I followed my instincts.

I could tell that mama was getting a little agitated. I know that she was burning up in that car because there wasn't an air conditioner in it. She started clearing her throat, letting me know that it was time for me to get my butt in the car.

"Can I call you sometime?" he asked, hoping that I wouldn't turn him down. How could I? He seemed so sincere. I wrote my number on the church bulletin that I stuck between the pages of my Bible, smiled, gave it to him, and climbed into Betsy. Mama looked at me trying to figure out what just happened. I shrugged my shoulders because I really didn't have a clue.

Angela Weathered

Visit 4

When I got home from church, I went into my room to change clothes.

"Shaneeka, telephone!" my grandmother yelled.

My heart began to pound louder and louder. I swear it was about to come out of my chest. I knew exactly who it was on the telephone, because I'd only given my number to one person, Eric.

When I got to the telephone, I tried to play the innocent role. It seemed kind of strange talking to a 'preacher's kid'. If I didn't know anything else about the bible, I knew you didn't want to make a man of God angry.

Our conversation was nice. I found out that he was a senior at Kendrick High School, he was into basketball, and that my beauty overcame him. With compliments like that, you would think he was out on a booty-call! As our conversation progressed, I realized that he was a sweet and interesting young man who seemed to really have his head on straight. I guess all that training he'd gotten in church all of his life had really paid off. He had dreams of someday becoming a lawyer. Not just any lawyer, but The Attorney General of the United States of America. He wanted to make a difference in people's lives. He seemed really sincere about what it was he wanted to do, and how he was going to go about doing it. I didn't doubt him one minute.

We had so much to talk about, and so little time to do it. As soon as I got home from school, he'd call me. Granny would have to make me get off the telephone so that I could get my homework and chores done before bedtime. The next Sunday, I joined the church. That allowed us to be able to spend a lot more time together. That wasn't the main reason I joined, but it did have something to do with it. He had a spiritual connection with God that I wanted to experience for myself. Yeah, I went to church throughout my life, but I didn't really understand my purpose for being there. He had so much knowledge, that I wanted him to share it with me.

He used words that I'd never heard of. Some would think he was just being a smart-ass, but he wasn't. He wanted more out of life, so he obtained as much knowledge as he could. He studied when everyone else wanted to play around. I admired that. If he said something, you could expect it to be done. Some smart people try to make others feel inferior because they don't know as much, but not Eric. We'd study for hours. He'd come over to my house, with my mother's blessings, and we'd get a bite to eat and hit the books. Since I moved, my grades started slipping, so he took it upon himself to make sure I came back up to above average.

After we finished studying, we'd go for walks around Carver Park, or take a couple of laps around the track at the school. I really enjoyed his company. It would seem that if you were around a person as much as we were, you would eventually get tired of them. It wasn't so in our situation. We complimented each other. It's almost as if we were joined at the hip or something.

We didn't mind spending all that time together, but his mother did. She felt as though we were too young to be so involved with one another. We should see other people; spread our wings. We were satisfied with the way things were.

I guess if she had someone in her life, she would have left us alone. Eric's father left her for a younger woman, and she acted as though she wanted everybody to be as miserable as she was. He'd been gone for over six years now. It seems like she would've found someone by then, but she hadn't. She got more pleasure out of harassing everyone else. Frankly, I don't think another man would put up with her messed up ways. I often wondered how someone as kind and loving as Eric could've come from a witch like her? God only knows.

Angela Weathered

Visit 5

It was May 16, 1985, a day I will never forget. I couldn't believe mama was letting me go on a date! She was very over protective. She and daddy went out on a date when she was fifteen years old. One thing lead to another, and nine months later my oldest sister was born. I guess she figured that if she could be so easily persuaded, then maybe I could be also. She knew that Eric was different though. He was in the church, and she considered him to be a well-mannered young man. Also, because we had a chaperone.

For my special evening, mama took me to the mall and bought me a new outfit. It was wonderful having my mother as my best friend. We'd finally worked through some of our problems. We still had a few minor ones that needed to be worked out, but that was okay. She knew how important this night would be for me, and she wanted to make sure it was perfect. She even let me wear a little lipstick. Some blush and a little bit of eyeshadow would have been nice, but I didn't want to press my luck.

Eric started off on the right foot, he showed up on time. It was kind of embarrassing though, because as soon as he walked in, my grandmother started snapping pictures. I can still hear her say, "That's a mighty fine boy you got there!" Eric's pink lips spread from one side of his face to the other.

We went to the movies and saw one of those horror flicks. I guess I was supposed to get scared and jump into his arms, but I didn't. I must admit, it might have been nice. From the movies, we went out to eat. It was very romantic.

The relationship that Eric and I shared was unreal. There was never any pressure about having sex. All he did was give me unconditional love. We'd go to the park, skating, or just sit around and talk all day. We had pure, clean fun.

It was time for Eric's prom, which they were having on the riverboat downtown. We sailed up and down the Chattahoochee River for several hours. The scent of love was in the air. For the first time in my life, I could truly say I was in love. I'd never felt as close to anyone as I felt to Eric that night. We slow danced to the soft music the band was playing. Eric wrapped his arms around me to keep me warm, and he kissed me softly. I started feeling things in places I never knew existed. He wasn't real muscular, but in his arms I felt safe. He was my king, and I, his queen.

The evening couldn't have been more perfect. That man was playing the mess out of that saxophone. Kenny G. didn't have anything on him. We must have danced five songs straight. I could tell he was getting excited, because I could feel his manhood start to rise. He slowly started to back away. From the expression on his face, I could tell that he was a little embarrassed.

After the cruise, we went back to my house. Eric always walked me to my door, but tonight was different. He led me past my door, straight back to the back of my apartment building. He began to kiss me passionately, as his hands roamed all over my body. I could feel his heart beating through his chest. All of a sudden, he just stopped.

He looked into my eyes and said, "This shouldn't have happened!"

I was a little confused. After all, we loved each other very much. I guess his conscience got the best of him. He believed strongly that you shouldn't have sex until you were married. I admired his views on pre-marital sex, but you can't get a sister all hot and bothered and then just back off. He thought it would be better for both of us if we just called it a night.

The next day he called me and apologized for the way he'd acted, and how he wanted our first time to be special. Any other guy would have taken advantage of the situation, but not Eric. He remained the perfect gentleman in my eyes.

Before ending our call, he said, "You are my Princess, and you deserve the best." From that night on, he called me "Princess".

Angela Weathered

Visit 6

It was our second anniversary together. Eric decided to make up a basket of food and have a picnic. We went to a park not to far from where I lived. It couldn't have been a more perfect day. The sun was just beginning to set. The rays from the sun beamed down, gently kissing my exposed shoulders softly. The wildflowers that surrounded the blanket released heavenly fragrances as the wind blew them gently. You could see the birds flying high in the sky, singing songs with beautiful melodies.

He'd gotten some grapes, strawberries, cheese, and a bottle of sparkling cider (since neither one of us was old enough to drink alcohol). As we drank from the champagne glasses, he stared into my eyes, as though he was looking into my soul. At that moment, he may well have been.

He leaned over and gently kissed me on my lips. At first, I was kind of reluctant to kiss him back. I didn't want to cause a brother to slip up, if you know what I mean. We were so into each other, that we didn't notice the little kids playing across the way, in the sandbox. That is, until they started laughing at us. It didn't matter to us. The whole world could have been watching, we still probably wouldn't have noticed.

A week after our picnic, Eric called me and told me that he had concerns about our future, and we needed to discuss them. It seems that his mother told him to stop seeing me. She suggested he focus more on his education than girls, because that's what should be important to him right now. If she had someone in her life, maybe she would stay out of ours, I thought. Although I felt that way, but I didn't say anything to him. I didn't want to become enemies with his mother. I didn't want to put him in the middle of anything like that. Just the thought of making him choose between the two of us made me sick to my stomach. Shame on his mother!

She stopped letting him use her car if he was coming to see me. One day I looked outside, and there he was. He'd dribbled his basketball all the way to my house. We lived atleast twelve miles apart. Now that's true love for you! Not only that, but he'd also written a song for me and recorded it on a cassette tape. He wanted me to have it that day, so that's why he came. Is that romantic or what! He wasn't very much of a singer, but to me, Luther Vandross didn't have a thing on him that day.

Tears of joy came streaming down my face. Before I knew it, I'd grabbed him and planted a big, wet one on his face. My mama came out onto the porch to see what all the commotion was about. I let her hear the song, and she cried too. It was hard for anyone not to cry. Sure, he could have just given me a tape with a song on it, but he thought enough of me to sit down and actually write one about me, about us. Was this some kind of dream I was having? I had to pinch myself to see for sure.

I was on cloud nine the rest of the day. Couldn't nobody tell me a thing. I was 'the girl'. I had a guy bending over backwards to satisfy me! That felt all right. He gave me unconditional love. The song was just one display of affection. That night, my special song must have played a dozen times. I couldn't count any further than that, because his words of love put me to sleep. I had wonderful dreams that night.

It seemed as though our love for each other was growing stronger by the day. The more our love grew, the more determined Eric's mother was to stop us from seeing each other. Even though we tried not to let it bother us, it did. It put more of a strain on Eric. Because I loved him so much, I didn't want him to feel as though he had to choose between us. That would have been a big mistake. Instead, I loved him enough to set him free. Too bad his mother couldn't have done the same. I stepped back from the situation and gave him the space he needed. Eventually, a choice had to be made. He chose his mother.

No, my life wasn't the same without him. In fact, I missed him dearly. There wasn't a day that went by that I didn't think about him. At the same time, I also thought about all of the pain that he allowed his mother to cause us. Four years and a broken heart later, we went our separate ways. Our parting was bittersweet.

Angela Weathered

Visit 7

In the wee hours of the night, I laid in my bed thinking about all of the things that I'd gone through with Eric. I was so deep in thought that I almost didn't hear my telephone ringing. I was all grown up now, so I had my own private telephone line connected in my bedroom.

"Hello," I said, talking just above a whisper. Mama had ears that could hear a pin dropping on snow, and I didn't want her all up in my business.

"Hey stranger!" the voice on the other end shouted.

"Who is this?" I asked because I couldn't catch the voice.

"Guess who?" he said being a real smart-ass.

By that time I began to get real irritated. I wasn't in the mood to be playing those silly ass-guessing games.

"Listen, it's two-a-damn-clock-in-the-morning, I don't have time to be playing no games!" I yelled into the receiver before I hung up. I just knew that mama would come knocking at my door any time now, but she didn't. A few seconds after I hung up, the phone rang again. I figured it was the same person I'd just hung up on. I figured they would realize that if they wanted to talk, they had better not play any games this time.

"Hello!" I said again. This time a little more curious about who was on the other end of the phone. Not too many people had my new number, but the ones that did have it wouldn't call my house that late at night playing games on the phone.

"Shaneeka, why you hang up on a brother?"

"Who is this?"

"This is Marcus. Don't tell me that you've already forgotten about me. Just think, I actually thought you loved me," he said laughing his ass off.

"Oh my god, it is you Marcus!" was all I could manage to get out because I was in a state of shock. He was the last person I would have thought was calling me. I didn't believe that I forgot what he sounded like. After all, this was my first love on the telephone.

"How have you been, Marcus?" I asked, showing genuine concern.

"I'm doing good. I just finished up my junior year at MSU, and I will be starting my internship in the fall at Saginaw General."

I was so proud of him at that very moment. He was doing exactly what he said he was going to do in so many of our childhood conversations. I wanted nothing more than to be able to report to him that, I too, was living out my childhood ambitions. That wasn't the case. My life, at that time, was in complete shambles.

"That's wonderful Marcus!"

"So, how are things going for my special lady?"

I went on to tell him my whole life's story since leaving Saginaw. He listened very attentively like so many times before. He was careful not to criticize me in any way. He did, however, get very upset about the fact that I hadn't kept in contact with him all those years.

"Shaneeka, how are we supposed to get married if we don't communicate with each other," he said coming at me from left field.

"What do you mean, Marcus?"

"I wasn't joking eight years ago, on April tenth, nineteen eighty-three, when I asked you to be my wife. I meant every word of it!"

My life was so messed up at that point that marriage was the last thing I wanted to be thinking about.

"All I can promise you, at this point, is that I will never lose contact with you again, my love, and that you will always hold a special place in my heart."

I could tell that he was smiling. I could hear his lips separate through the telephone receiver.

"Well that's fair enough, now take my number down and don't hesitate to call me if you ever need me.....for anything."

I took his number down and we bid each other farewell. I fell fast asleep.

It had only been two months since my breakup with Eric, but it seemed like much longer. After almost five years of being with someone, you get kind of use to them. When you can practically finish a person's sentence, or know what they're thinking without saying a word, you have something really special.

There were so many reminders of him throughout our apartment. I needed to get rid of them, but I couldn't. After all, most of the times we'd shared together were good. They weren't gifts that an ordinary person would think of, they were unique. He never did give me a ring. He said we didn't need one.

"Princess, we have that special ring around our hearts!"

Some people would've thought he was just being cheap, not me. I'd rather have true love, than gifts any day. Gifts can be taken away or destroyed, but true love lasts forever. I ended up keeping them. I put the gifts in a box and stored it on my closet shelf.

I decided that I need to get my priorities back in order, so once again, I started going back to church. Maybe my relationship had gone sour because of my lack of obedience to God's word. I'd turned my back on God. Atleast, that's how I felt.

We were having a "Holy-Ghost" revival all week long, and I made it a point to be there every night. The preacher was from Illinois, and our minister wanted the congregation to come out and show our support. I sat on the third pew as usual. When Minister Smith got up, he introduced his entire family that had come with him. It was like an instant replay. His oldest son was sitting there playing the organ, and looking directly at me. I wasn't about to fall for that mess again. I got up and moved to the back of the church. The devil is a liar!

After service was over, I tried to get out of the church as fast as I could. Just as I was about to exit the building, my preacher's daughter, Tammy, stopped me. I stood and talked with her for a few minutes, and you-know-who walked up. She introduced us and left. That winch!

"Hi my name is Tyreek," he said all sure of himself. He just knew that I wanted to know who he was. He was doing me a favor by allowing me to be in his presence. Give me a break. I wasn't ready for no tired-ass-wanna-be brother with lame conversation. All he probably talked about was himself anyway. He just stood there looking at me; waiting for me to say something. I saw other people starting to gather around us, so I tried to be on my best behavior. I spoke because I didn't want to be rude. I told him my name and said goodbye.

When I got home, Tammy called me and told me that Tyreek was interested in me and wanted to know if he could have my telephone number.

"You have got to be kidding me, right?" I said before I even realized it.

She talked about how nice of a person he was, and how she'd known him for almost twenty years.

"Just give him a try girl, it's not like you have guys beating down your door!" she said with a snap.

I gave in. The least I could do was talk to him since he went through all the trouble of trying to get my number. I told her to go ahead and give it (my number) to him. A few seconds later he was on the telephone. He must have been standing right next to her the whole time.

Tyreek was twenty years old, had a jherri curl. I guess he probably weighed about two-thirty. Just like Eric, he was so-so looking. He was in college studying to become a computer programmer and also played the organ for a church on Sundays. The boy really knew how to dress! I had to give him that much.

He told me about how he'd recently had his heart broken, and how he wanted a friend to talk to. If anything else evolved from it, then that was fine with him. With him being so far away, conversation is all we'd be sharing. Maybe this was the answer to both of our problems. I still wasn't quite over Eric, but I had to move on for my own sake.

I let him know straight up exactly how I felt about mama's boys and sex. I explained to him that I was a virgin when I met him, and that I planned on staying one until the day I got married. What I wasn't expecting, though, was his response.

"That's okay, I'm a virgin too!" he said.

That simply blew my world. A twenty-year-old male-virgin? You could have sold me for a nickel! The next thing that went through my mind was, maybe he's gay. Wouldn't that be something?

He seemed like a nice guy. He loved to pamper me with materialistic things. This, I wasn't use to. Sure, Eric gave me a lot of emotional support, but getting diamonds and gold was quite nice. After knowing him only three days, Tyreek gave me a gold necklace with the letter "T" on it. One month to the day, I received a diamond ring. He must have really wanted some, because every time you looked around, he was giving me something.

All the rest of that week, Tyreek treated me like a queen. I was on cloud nine. Eric was a thing of the past, and I was finally moving on with my life. It felt wonderful. Tyreek was heading back to Illinois, but he wanted to keep our relationship going even though we lived so far apart.

"Absence makes the heart grow fonder," he said.

I decided to give it a try. This way, I wouldn't have someone constantly smothering me. He'd be able to have his freedom, and I, mine.

It had only been a week since I'd last seen Tyreek, but it seemed like much longer. I was sitting downstairs at my grandmother's house when the doorbell rang. When I opened the door, all I saw was a big vase of red roses. I should've known who they were from. After all, surprises were his style.

Visit 8

It was the day before Tyreek was to arrive in Columbus, so I wanted to plan something special. Maybe a walk along the lake or something. I was so anxious that night that I could barely sleep. I had two months worth of loneliness built up inside of me.

As usual, he arrived on time. I ran out to the car before he could turn the engine off good. He'd changed so much. He finally cut that jerri curl off and was now wearing a box. It made him look a lot better.

That night, we went to the park and had a picnic. Tyreek had a look on his face like he wanted to say something. To be honest, I was afraid to ask him what was wrong. As curious as I was, I decided to go for it.

He looked me dead in my eyes and said, "Baby, it's been almost a year since we met, and I've grown to love you so much."

After he cleared the lump from his throat, he continued.

"Being here with you tonight made me realize how much I really do love you and need you in my life."

By that time, my heart was working overtime. He pulled a tiny crystal box out of his pocket and handed it to me. I was so nervous that I started to cry. This time, they were tears of joy! It was the most beautiful ring I'd ever seen. It had a three-carat, heart shaped diamond surrounded by smaller ones.

"Will you marry me?" he asked in a tone almost as though he couldn't believe he was asking me himself.

Naturally I said yes. I mean, what else could I say with that big diamond starring me in the face.

It started getting dark, so we decided to leave the park. Tyreek needed to change clothes, so we stopped by his hotel room. He opened the door, and when I walked in, I saw the sheets turned back, with rose petals all over them. There was a bottle of red wine on the nightstand, along with some fruit. I began to get nervous because I knew what he had in mind. He made it clear to me that I was who he wanted as his wife by giving me the ring. It was only natural that our relationship moved to the next level.

"I know all of this is new to you. It's new to me as well," he said, moving closer to me. He kept his eyes locked on mine as he came over and sat next to me on the bed. My heart started to pound so loud, I'm sure he heard it. Before I could say a word, he had his lips planted onto mine. We'd both waited so long for this night to happen, but now that it was, I was scared as hell. I felt myself slowly being lowered onto the bed. He unbuttoned my blouse with one hand, while the other one roamed freely all over my body. I didn't resist, because I knew that deep inside, I wanted him too! When all of my clothes were off, I laid back onto the bed, shaking uncontrollably.

"Just relax, its going to be okay," he said. That was easy for him to say.

As he laid down on top of me, I remembered that I wasn't taking any birth control. After all, this wasn't supposed to be happening.

"Tyreek, I don't want to get pregnant," I said in a trembling voice.

"You won't, I promise," he responded, holding up his two 'scout's honor' fingers.

Before he could get the word promise out good, I felt this excruciating pain. The act of sensitive tissues being torn apart for the very first time. I tried to relax, but I couldn't. It hurt so bad! I didn't understand how people enjoyed doing it. I'd hoped that when he saw the pain in my eyes, he would stop. It wasn't so. I looked at him, only to realize that he had his eyes closed. He was in another world. All I could think about was how glad I'd be when this was all over.

After he was finished, he rolled over onto the bed next to me. He lifted me up into his arms and held me close.

"You felt so good," he said. Too bad I couldn't say the same to him. Don't get me wrong, the thought of making love with him felt good, just not the physical part of it. Maybe it won't always be like that. I closed my eyes and fell asleep in his arms.

I couldn't believe that I'd finally lost my virginity. I think I was one of the only virgins left in the twelfth grade. At last, I felt as though I'd finally become a woman. Tyreek's woman! Oh yeah, I could tell by the way that he fumbled through the whole act, that he probably was telling me the truth about his being a virgin too.

Angela Weathered

Visit 9

Tyreek and I had been together for two years now. We decided to get married in July, so I started planning early. Mama and me went to the print shop and ordered the invitations. Just think, in a couple of months, I'll be Mrs. Tyreek Anthony Smith! I like the way that sounds. I went to be fitted for my wedding gown. God, there were so many to choose from. One thing was for sure; it had to be snow white. Nobody had to know my little secret.

After a long day of running around, I had to get home so I wouldn't miss Tyreek's call. He never did call that day. As a matter of fact, with everything going on, I hadn't noticed that he hadn't called in a couple of days. I felt as though I'd better call to see what was going on. I didn't want to jump to conclusions, but it was kind of hard not to. Was he getting cold feet? I didn't want to speculate, so I called him.

He was responsible for getting our household set up since I agreed that I would be the one relocating. This was the reason he gave as to why he hadn't talked to me in a couple of days. He wanted everything to be just right when I got there. I accepted his reasoning without question.

Since my mom was paying for our wedding, we thought that it would be better for us to get married in Columbus. This would allow us to be married in the place we first set eyes on each other. It had great sentimental value to us. We began our relationship there, now we'd be beginning a lifetime together there.

I, like many others I'm sure, started having second thoughts about marriage. I started to feel like I was too young to settle down. Every time I started to feel this way, I began to think of the love that I had in my heart for Tyreek, and then everything would be okay. I would settle down. He was everything I wanted in a husband and more. Was I truly over Eric? It seemed like the closer it got to my wedding day, the more I thought about him. How was my getting married going to effect him? Was I doing this to get back at him for choosing his mother over me? Was this marriage a rebound thing? Was Tyreek experiencing the same kinds of feelings?

I decided that before I went any further, I needed to talk to someone for proper guidance. I called my pastor up and expressed my concerns. The last thing I wanted to do was have my marriage end up like mama and daddy's did. I wouldn't wish that on my worst enemy.

Reverend Taylor told me that it was normal to have those feelings before getting married. If you truly loved someone, that wouldn't be a reason to call off the wedding. I wish Tyreek had thought like that.

After four days of trying to get in contact with Tyreek, he finally returned my telephone call.

"Hey baby, I'm sorry it took me so long to get back to you. I've been very busy," he said like that was going to make everything all right.

"Come on Tyreek!" I said, getting really frustrated with him.

"You can come up with something better than that!" I continued.

"I'm just trying to get everything set up before you get here."

He was still sticking to his story. That was one thing about him, he was very careful to make his lies seem real. He could keep his lies straight. But I knew Tyreek, and I knew that from the sound of his voice, he wasn't being honest with me.

"Now look Tyreek! Just be real with me. If you aren't ready to get married let me know. Don't have me going down the isle, only to get divorced a couple months later. You know how sacred marriage is to me. Marriage means something, and if you aren't ready, then don't do it."

"Naw baby, it ain't like that! You know I love you! I've just been having some doubts lately. Getting married is a big step".

Like I didn't know that. He must have really thought I was stupid or something.

"Oh, and you are just now figuring out that you were having these feelings, two weeks before the wedding?" I yelled.

"Shaneeka, I do love you. I'm just scared. All of these thoughts have been going through my mind, and I'm just not so sure I'm ready to get married."

I was real upset with him. I'd been trying to reach him for weeks, and now he waits until the last minute to tell me he's not ready. I completely lost it!

"Were you just going to let me march down the isle, and find that you stood me up? Is that all I meant to you? You were definitely certain that you wanted to marry me while you were laying up between my legs taking my virginity, weren't you?" I gave him the dial tone.

A few seconds later, the telephone rang again, but I didn't answer. With every ring, I felt a sharp pain prick my heart, as though it were a knife. Finally, there were no more rings.

He left message after message about how sorry and confused he was. He went on about how he needed a little more time to get himself together. He knew what he wanted when he laid his sorry ass on top of me. He didn't second-guess that decision, did he! I said I wasn't gone trip off no shit like that, but the more I thought about it, the more pissed off I got. What's the big deal, either you love someone or you don't. You either want to be with them or you don't. It's that simple. No if's, and's, or but's about it.

I was not going to beg anyone to marry me. Some lucky guy would have me as his wife, eventually. In the meantime, what was I going to do with all of the stuff that I bought for the wedding? I called as many people as I could to let them know. I couldn't take my wedding dress back because I'd had it altered to fit me perfectly. I had to place an ad in the newspaper. Someone could get better use out of it than I did.

The dress sold within a couple of weeks, so that was a big relief. We used the reception napkins as toilet paper. They served a much better purpose than I'd bought them for! Mama and me ate little bite-sized sausages for breakfast, lunch, and dinner. Waste not, want not. So it wasn't a total loss.

I needed to do something to get my mind off things. I ended up going to Seafood Bar & Grill getting a job. It wasn't the greatest one, but it was a start. I knew I wasn't ready to go to nobody's college, and the military was definitely out of the question. This would allow me the chance to make a little spending money. It wasn't like I had any bills. I was still living at home with mama, and I was able to spend the money I made as I saw fit.

While working at Seafood Bar & Grill, I met a girl, or shall I say lady, named Veronica. She told everyone to call her Ronnie because "Veronica" made her feel like an old lady. She was twenty-six years old, light-skinned with red hair, and very down to earth. Our personalities cliqued almost immediately, and we became real good friends. We called ourselves the "SBG Crew". Most of the time, if we weren't working, we all hung out together. We were definitely a force to be reckoned with. The other girls at work were always talking about going out to the clubs and meeting all these fine guys. Since I was only eighteen (I was the baby of the crew), I couldn't get in any of them, legally.

Ronnie came up to me one night and asked me if I wanted to go out with them. She explained to me that she knew the bouncer and that I wouldn't have any problem getting in. I was down for that. Later after work, we headed over to her house to change clothes. She and I were about the same size, so I borrowed an outfit from her. We put our little makeup on. Shoot, we were ready for the world. On our way to City Lights (this club was the bomb!), we stopped by the mall and put on some expensive perfume they had on display in Gayfers. Hey, what can I say, we were broke!

When we got to the club, they were jamming. M.C. Hammer pumping it up! The dance floor was too crowded, and the tables were full, so we grabbed a seat at the bar. Ronnie ordered her usual slow gin fizz. She never would finish the whole thing. She'd just sip on it all night long. I ordered an 'almost-virgin fuzzy navel'. They made those drinks strong as hell! That's why I always requested mine the way that I did. We sat at the bar and waited on the rest of the crew to show up.

It wasn't long before the guys started sweating us. Ronnie had her shades on like she was cool. That was her way of checking out the guys on the down low. She spotted this dark skinned brother standing by the stage, and she practically had her tongue hanging out of her mouth.

"Girl, you see that guy standing over there in the black? He's too fine!" she shouted.

"He's OK," I said. "Girl, It looks like he's coming over here too."

Before Ronnie could get a word out of her mouth good, the guy was at the bar asking me to dance. I couldn't turn him down. I looked at Ronnie and smiled as I walked to the dance floor.

"You bitch!" she shouted with a little smirk on her face.

When I got back to the bar, we had a good laugh. I excused myself to go to the restroom. On the way there, I spotted this want-to-be-player named Cedrick. He was someone I would talk to on the telephone if I was really bored. As I walked by him, I told him what my drink preference was. When I got back to the bar, the waiter had already brought it over.

I should've known that Cedrick wouldn't do anything without wanting something in return. He brought his sweaty behind over to the bar trying to get next to me. I tried to be nice, but it was hard to do with him. He wanted to dance, I didn't. I gave in though. I figured it was worth the one drink he bought me. I danced one song with him and that was it. When I got back to the bar, it was kind of late, so we called it a night. I was feeling kind of tipsy, so I wasn't going to drive home. Cedrick offered to give me a ride, and I accepted. With much reluctance, might I add.

Instead of taking me home, he took me to his apartment. I knew I should've followed my first instinct. He was going to try to take advantage of the situation. We went and sat down on his bed to watch television. He started changing his clothes. I just ignored him. He didn't have much going on, and what little he did have, I wasn't interested in. He came over and sat next to me on the bed in his boxer shorts. Like he really turned me on. He started kissing me on my neck. I was more interested in the show that was on.

He kissed me in my mouth. It was on then. I had to show him a thing or two. Before he could go any further, I jumped up and ran to the bathroom. I guess all that alcohol I drunk finally caught up with me. I must have thrown up about five minutes straight. That must have really ruined his mood, because he didn't touch me after that. I told him that I thought it would be better if he took me home. He agreed.

It's not that Cedrick was such a terrible person or anything, it's just that he was so possessive. He had to know where I was all of the time. If I told him I had to work, he'd show up at my job to make sure that I was there. If I was at home, he'd want to talk on the telephone until it was too late for me to go anywhere. I guess his being so possessive, and the fact that he was a terrible lover completely turned me off.

Cedrick and I had only been together twice, but that was one time too many. The brother was hung like a pimple! He knew he was too.

"It's not the size of the boat, it's the motion in the ocean," he said.

I guess he'd been told about his too-small member before. Not only was he not very well endowed, but he couldn't use the little that he had either.

He invited me over to his house for dinner to set the mood. I must admit, I was definitely impressed with the setup he'd prepared. You could tell he put a lot of effort into the meal. Cedrick claimed that he was from Jamaica and was always listening to Reggae music, so I wasn't surprised by all of the Islander dishes that he'd prepared.

He had the table setup with nice crystal wineglasses, red rose petals about the table, and the lights were turned down low. We ate dinner by candlelight. During dinner, we had some interesting conversation. He talked about his future goals of becoming a police officer and how he wanted to be financially secure before getting married.

"I want nothing but the best for my wife and children", he said with a big smile of his face.

He seemed to have every detail of his life all figured out. I should've given him the benefit of doubt.

There was no intimacy involved with our departure from the dinning room or our arrival into his bedroom. He removed his clothes and jumped into his bed. I just stood there, dumbfounded, fully clothed, looking at him. He patted the bed with his hand and asked me to join him. That sucker! He didn't have a romantic bone in his body. I wanted this to hurry up and be over, so I took off my clothes and climbed into bed next to him. Here goes nothing.

He kissed me one time and climbed on top of me. It was so pitiful; I just laid there, hoping that it would soon be over.

"You feel so good to me," he said over and over again.

Finally with a loud groan, his body went stiff and he rolled over next to me on the bed.

"That was good, wasn't it", he said.

I could've lied, like I'm sure the other women that he'd bedded had done to him, but I wouldn't give him the satisfaction.

"I've had better," I responded. Like I had so much experience myself, right? In fact, the only other person I'd been with was Tyreek. He wasn't much better than Cedrick though.

If I was a smoker, I would have lit a cigarette and smoked it while he was humping me.

"That's kind of a rude thing to say, don't you think?" he came back kind of upset with me.

I'm sorry, but his lovin was whack, and ain't no way I was going to boost his ego by lying to him. He didn't even attempt to give me any satisfaction. It was all about him. As far as I was concerned, I was doing him a favor by being honest with him.

Afterwards, he climbed out of bed and went and took a shower. He just left me lying there, butt naked, without saying a word. He didn't offer me a drink of water or anything. I guess he must have cooled off when he was in the shower, because when he came out, his attitude had completely changed. When he came back into the room, he wanted to go for round number two. I don't think so!

"I'm not feeling this, Cedrick. Let's just pretend that this never happened, okay?" I replied and turned to leave the room.

I knew what he had in mind when he invited me over for dinner, so I came prepared. I grabbed my overnight bag and disappeared into the bathroom. He followed me and sat on the toilet while I showered.

While in the shower I thought about what had just happened. The more I thought about it, the more pissed off I became.

"How dare he climb on top of me like some wild animal in heat and do his duty I thought.

I grabbed for the towel, but it fell into the water, that made me even more pissed off. After I dried off, I walked back into his bedroom with him following close behind.

"I'm ready to go," I yelled. "I want to get the hell up out of here right now!"

"You know you really hurt my feelings a little while ago," he said sounding pitiful.

He kept mumbling about something and finally I just snapped.

"You know what Cedrick, you can kiss my ass! You are the sorriest excuse for a lover I have ever seen. You talking about how I hurt your feelings, hell you hurt mine by pulling out that little two inch dick of yours, talking about making me climb the walls." I was on now!

I was just so sick and tired of the brothers always talking about how big their thang's were and how they can make love to you all night long, when, in all actuality, they don't last longer than fifteen minutes on a good night. They were just giving you a lot of lip service. You finally give them a chance to prove themselves and their theories to you, and you end up disappointed. Then he's off to the next unsuspecting sistah. I wasn't even going to help his ego out like that. He got the right one this time.

"Yeah you made me climb the walls all right, but not because it was feeling soooo good, but because I was trying to get away from your pitiful butt!"

I grabbed my clothes, got dressed and left. The nerve of him. Talking about I hurt his feelings, yeah right!

On my way home, I had myself a good time laughing about his sorry ass. World's greatest lover my butt! I actually felt sorry for him because I knew that he actually believed he was good. He actually thought that he was doing something while he was on top of me. Just wait until I tell Ronnie about this. I couldn't wait to get to work that night. Just as I figured, she was rolling.

"A good laugh was all I got out of it," I said.

She encouraged me to give him another try. "You know guys go through this shit sometimes. Maybe it's been a while since he had some, and he got a little anxious".

Why was she trying to take up for this idiot and his sorry lovemaking skills?

"I'm not taking up for him either. Things like that just happen sometimes," she said.

After much thought, I decided to call him and apologize for my actions. Maybe I did get a little carried away. We decided to give it another try. After work, I went back over to his place. I must admit, he had a lot of courage to step back up to the plate again with the risk of striking out big time.

He turned down the lights and put on some soft Reggae music. Some things will never change. This time, he wanted to undress me, so I let him. As he laid me back onto his bed, I could feel him trembling. I didn't say a word. He began to kiss me all over my body. Now this was more like it, I thought to myself. He seemed to be getting frustrated because his member was not responding to my body.

"Let me try something okay," he said without waiting for a response.

He moved quickly to my thighs, spread them apart, and slid his tongue deep into my womanhood. Damn it felt good! He worked miracles with his tongue. Why didn't he do this the first time? My body started to tremble as the fire within me began to burn deeper. I felt the lava deep inside of me building, about to explode. I couldn't hold back anymore. My hips were swaying from side to side as I held the back of his head so he could get closer to my love spot. With rhythmic thrusts, I felt my peak explode. I let out a loud groan, no longer able to maintain my composure. My body lay shivering as though I was having a seizure.

When he climbed on top of me, I could see that he was now erect and ready to go. He wiggled around until he was inside of me. With only a few quick thrusts, he reached his climax. I guess he was so excited about finally pleasing me, that he was turned on as well. I have to admit this was a huge improvement from our encounter on yesterday. Maybe he had potential after all. Maybe.

Sunday afternoons, hundreds of people rode through Baker Village Park. Some parked, while others drove around going about five mph, hanging out of the windows yelling the first thing that came to their minds. All of the GQ's (ghetto queens) came out. You'd see them with their high, multi-colored hair and mini-skirts up to their you-know-what. The brothers wore their hats tilted to the side, with a mouth full of gold teeth, trying to holler at anything that would let them.

Ronnie and I parked under a shade tree and sat on the hood of the car. All the guys that drove by were checking us out. You know we had to play hard to get. This guy drove up next to us and parked his car. He was very nice looking. His name was Michael. He was stationed out at Fort Benning. Yes, he was a soldier. I vowed to myself that I would never to get involved with a soldier. Don't get me wrong, there wasn't anything wrong with soldiers. I just didn't want to get emotionally involved with someone and, within a few months, have to transfer and leave me all alone once again. So I made up my mind that I was keeping that vow.

Michael asked me if we could get together later on that evening, but I told him that I already had plans with my girlfriends. We were going out to the NCO club on the base. I let him know that if I just happened to run into him out there, it would be OK. That was the end of our conversation. He drove away.

"Girl, that nigga ain't no good! He tried to sweat me at the club the other night. Now he gone walk up here like he don't even know who I am and shit!" Ronnie said.

That was a side of her I'd never seen before. Was she just jealous? I mean it's not like I was about to run off and marry him tomorrow or anything. I simply let it go. I refused to go there with her.

Another guy across the street threw his hand up and motioned for me to come over there where he was. I told Ronnie to watch my back, and I slowly eased over to him.

His name was Xavier. And guess what, he was a soldier also. This was a trip!

"Was that your boy I saw you with a few minutes ago?" he asked.

I didn't answer his question. It wasn't any of his damn business. I gave him that "e-x-c-u-s-e me look. I guess he could tell I wasn't going put up with no stuff, because his tone of voice changed almost instantly. He asked me if he could take me out to dinner that night, but I told him that my girls and me were hanging out. I mentioned where and left it at that. Ronnie had to be to work in an hour, so we had to roll.

Visit 10

When we got to the club that night, it was crowded. Ronnie and I were sitting at the table swaying with the beat of the music. I looked over towards the door hoping to see Michael, but I didn't. Instead, I saw Xavier. I tried to hide, but he'd already seen me. As he made his way over to the table, I gave him a smile. He offered to buy me a drink, and I definitely wasn't going to turn him down. Luckily there was a long line at the bar.

While he was getting my drink, Michael showed up. I didn't know what to do. I didn't tell Xavier to come, so why should I feel guilty? I tried to rationalize the situation to keep my conscience clear. I didn't tell him to meet me at the club so we could get better acquainted. I told him that I was hanging out with my girls. It was his decision to come, so he just had to deal with whatever happened.

The music was awesome. Michael asked me to dance, so we went to the dance floor. We must have danced a good five songs straight. I was dancing so hard and having so much fun, I didn't even see Xavier standing by the dance floor with my coke in his hand. I shrugged my shoulders as if I was saying "you snooze, you loose!" He simply walked away. I actually felt kind of bad.

I was about to lead Michael off the dance floor as Keith Sweat started begging his butt off. Michael stopped me in my tracks and pulled me close to him. I didn't know the first thing about slow dragging, and I let him know it.

"I'll teach you," he said, and held me closer.
"Just follow my lead," he whispered into my ear.
It wasn't so bad after all. God he smelled good! I could feel it all down in my "G" zone. To top it off, he started singing the song in my ear. Honey, if he could make love half as good as he could dance and sing, I'd found myself a winner!

After we finished our dance, I went to the ladies room to freshen up. On my way back to the table, Xavier came up behind me and whispered in my ear.

"You scrub!"

I didn't know what that meant, but I was sure that he wasn't giving me a compliment. I smiled and continued to walk back to my table. Michael was waiting patiently. After we left the club, it was customary to stop at Krystal's or Denny's to get a bite to eat since they were the only two places open at that time of morning.

When we pulled up in the parking lot of my apartment complex, Michael turned his car off. We had nice conversation for a while, but it was getting late. I gave him my telephone number, and told him to give me a call. He leaned over to kiss me, and I didn't try to stop him. Not only a good dancer, but kisser as well. Not that I had many people to compare him to. His tongue felt so good in my mouth. The taste of his warm juices sent chills up and down my spine. I began to feel my womanhood start to pulsate, as he slowly caressed the back of my neck with his hand. His breathing started to intensify as his tongue made tiny circles in my mouth. With his free hand, he began to caress my breast. It felt so good, I could feel my nipples become erect immediately. I reached inside of his shirt and began to rub his hairy chest. Damn! That really turned me on. I began to work my way down to his manhood. Whoa! The brother was hung! "Snap out of it Shaneeka" I just kept trying to tell myself, but my hormones were racing out of control, and I needed some good lovin. If his kisses were any indication of what kind of lover he was, then I was definitely in for a treat.

Right at that moment Tyreek popped into my mind, and all of my desires faded. How could I just jump into something like that all over again? I didn't want to hurt Michael, and I sure as hell didn't want to be hurt all over again, so I asked him to stop. I had to back off and let the brother know, right then and there, that this wasn't that kind of party. He apologized. I accepted.

He called me the next day wanting to get together for lunch. I cleared my schedule. We went to grab a bite to eat. After that, we went out to Cooper Creek Park and parked next to the water. As the sun started going down, it looked so beautiful. You could see the sun's reflection on the water as the ducks swam past. Michael lifted the trunk and turned on the radio. "Make it last forever" was jamming. At this rate, I wanted it to last forever. We began to slow dance to the music. I remembered what he'd taught me. For the average person looking at us, they'd swear we were having sex in the upright position. We went back to his barracks room. It was set up kind of nice. He had a net hanging from the ceiling. What that was for, I don't know. He lit a candle and dimmed the lights. He put on soft music in the background. The mood was on! He removed my shoes and began to massage my feet. I thought I was in heaven. He had some wine in the little refrigerator in his room, so he poured us a glass. He took a sip... I took a sip... he took a sip.

He guided me to my feet, and we began to dance slowly. It seemed like every time we were together, Keith Sweat would come on the radio. He began to kiss me on my neck softly. It felt rather nice. I could feel his heart beating faster and faster. I could tell he was getting hot, because his member started poking me. I felt myself reach up and start undressing him. Hell, if a man can take charge, so can I! I wasn't ashamed to admit that I wanted him.

He led me to his bed as he finished undressing me. "Are you on birth control?" he asked.

Atleast he practices safe sex, I thought. He kissed me from the crown of my head, to the sole of my feet. He made love to my WHOLE body!

He slowly slid his tongue into my earlobe. The warmth of his thick tongue made me wet. As he began to unbutton my shirt, he pulled me closer to him as if he never wanted to let me go. As our clothes fell to the floor, he laid me down onto the bed. By this time, Keith was singing "Let me hear you tell me you want me..." as though he was reading my mind. I wanted this man bad.

He began to run his tongue down the center of my breast, then to my stomach, making little love circles along the way. When he reached my navel, he took his hands and slowly moved my legs apart, placing one leg on each of his shoulders. The warmth of his tongue pressed softly against my inner thighs. When his thick tongue touched my tiny jewel, I felt shutters deep inside of me. I began to rock my hips back and forth to meet the groove that he created with his shoulders. I could feel the fire burning inside of me. My head began to sway from side to side uncontrollably. I felt myself being elevated to a new level of sensual excitement. As I began to reach my climax, a deep groan came from deep within my throat. It was wonderful.

When Michael resurfaced, he had a look of intensity on his face. He smoothly worked his way back on top of me, placing his manhood deep inside of me, all in one motion. His thrusts were so controlled and intense and with every movement, our bodies were in sync. The smell of sex was throughout the room as we both reached our peak. It was the second one for me that night. I fell back into his arms; exhausted from the love we'd just made.

He had me whipped the very first time. I could deal with that kind of lovin! The kind with no strings attached. Maybe it sounds like I'm a slut, but men have been doing it for years. I wasn't going into this relationship with any expectations, that way, I wouldn't get hurt. It was like our bodies belonged together. As he would say, we fit like a glove. He nicknamed my womanhood "The Love Cove". Although I wouldn't mind being his lady, I wanted to come and go as I please. Michael, on the other hand was looking for a commitment. He said he'd done everything he wanted to do, played all of the games that he wanted to play, and now it was time for him to settle down. That scared me. All of my life, I've wanted someone to want me like that, and now I have the chance to have it. All of the crap I had to deal with made me put up a shield. It's almost like my heart just went cold when it came to men. I wanted them only when it was convenient for me. I was in control of the situation. For once in my life, I made all the moves. I kind of felt sorry for Michael, because what he wanted, and what I was going to give him were two totally different things.

I talked to Michael earlier in the day, and he told me to come and visit him later on that night. He had barracks duty and couldn't leave. When I got there, he was still in his uniform, so we went upstairs to his room so he could change. While undressing, he told me that he had a surprise for me.

"I saw something at the Post Exchange today that reminded me of you, and I just had to get it."

As he was talking, he went into the refrigerator. This move threw me completely off. Just as I was about to ask him what he was talking about, he pulled out a strawberry about the size of an apple.

"When I saw this, it reminded me of "The Love Cove", big, sweet, and juicy."

All I could do was laugh. We ate it together, one bite after another. He popped in the movie "Shaka Zulu" and we laid back and relaxed.

Michael's company was going to California for thirty days to do field exercises, so I went out to visit him before he left. We sat in the car and said our good-byes. It was a rather sad day for the both of us. Although I'd made up in my mind that I wasn't going to develop any feelings for him, I found myself doing just that. Was I really in love with him, or was it the love that he made to me? That was the question I had to ask myself even to this day.

Visit 11

With Michael gone for the next several weeks, I figured it would be a good time to go and hang out with my girls. City Lights was getting played out, so we decided to go to Richardson's Lounge. I tried not to hang out there too much, because every time you looked around, somebody was getting shot in there. It was a little hole-in-the-wall club, but the atmosphere was the bomb. They served some chicken wings that made you want to slap your mama.

Ronnie and me found a table close to the dance floor, which was unusual, because those were the first ones to fill up. They had a talent show every weekend, with the same tired people, singing the same tired songs. I got up to go to the bathroom, and as I passed the door, I saw Xavier coming in. He was polite. Considering our last encounter.

"What's up scrub?" He said, as he passed by.

I really couldn't blame him for acting this way. After all, I did kind of diss him the last time I saw him. I felt like I owed it to him, so I invited him to join us at our table. He came.

Last night wasn't so bad, and neither was Xavier. I guess I just didn't give him a chance. If nothing else, he'd make a nice friend. He called me and asked me if I wanted to go and shoot some hoops. It wouldn't really be considered a date, right. I mean, we were just going to shoot the ball around a little bit and grab a bite to eat. It would be strictly platonic.

I'd never really looked at him in a sexual kind of way, but he was actually quite attractive. He was a little bit older than I would have chosen (thirty-three), but like they say age ain't nothing but a number. Besides, he didn't look old.

The last couple of days, I really enjoyed his company. We went out to a movie and stopped at Denny's on the way back home. When we finally got finished, it was almost four o'clock in the morning. I didn't want to hear my mama's mouth, so I decided that I would spend the night at his house. He was a perfect gentleman, which surprised me. I slept in his guestroom and he in the other. In the morning, I was awakened by the sweet smell of breakfast cooking.

After breakfast, I showered and got dressed. He let me borrow one of his jogging suits since I didn't have any clothes of my own to put on. We listened to some music and just chilled. Before I knew it, it was four hours later which meant I had to be to work soon. He dropped me off at home, gave me a quick peck on the cheek, and left.

All during the time I was at work, I couldn't stop thinking about the time we'd spent together. No pressure, just fun. I made up in my mind that he was definitely a keeper. We could be friends. When I went on break, I decided to give him a call. He wasn't home, so I left him a message saying I'd like to see him later on. He must have gotten my message, because he came through the drive-thru at Seafood Bar & Grill and confirmed our 'little date'.

After work, I went home, showered, and headed over to his house. He cooked a nice dinner of steak, baked potatoes, and some kind of vegetable I'd never heard of. It was the bomb. He was into meditation and he had all kinds of oils and incense. He lit candles throughout the house and turned down the lights. I was given a bathrobe to put on so that I could relax and be comfortable. He poured us both a glass of wine to drink as the music played. He kneeled down behind me and gently eased the bathrobe off my shoulders, kissing each one softly. He began to pour the warm oil into his hands and rub it gently over my shoulders. It felt so good being pampered like that. To feel the warm oil run through my toes, down my back, and other places I dare not mention, was breath taking. I felt his soft lips on my neck, working their way down my body. Something inside of me just melted. I erased all thoughts from my mind. He told me to concentrate on here and now. I didn't have a problem with that. With every breath in my body, I wanted him, and I wanted him then. He made me wait. He had a little freak in him. He did things to me that I'd only heard about (and some I hadn't). He took me to another level of ecstasy. It felt so good that I got cramps in my toes from curling theme every time that he touched me. The sweat was dripping from our bodies as though a faucet had been turned on.

Xavier got on his knees behind me on the floor and began to massage my shoulders. He put some fragranced oil on my neck and down my back so that he could work my muscles good. He blew soft kisses in the places that he touched. He laid me down softly on my stomach and poured the remaining oil in the center of my back. He gently straddled me as he worked his way down to my butt, thighs, and calves. I could feel his erection growing.

As he leaned forward to turn me over, I saw something in him that I'd never seen before. The warmth in his eyes told me that he wanted more than just sex, he wanted me completely. We just stared at each other for a few moments as if we were searching each other's souls. I felt a connection with him that almost frightened me.

He kissed me softly on my neck and slowly worked his way to my breasts. He worked like a skilled artist creating a masterpiece. Unable to control himself any longer, he guided his manhood into my depths, and with rhythmic thrusts, we both reached our climax simultaneously. Tonight, I had multiple orgasms. Who said you can't teach an old dog new tricks. This one knew all the latest moves.

Was I starting to fall in love with Xavier? Could that be possible, or was I just trying to make up for the loneliness of not being with Michael? With Xavier I felt so carefree, unlike with Michael, but I was in love with Michael. He was my soul mate. Maybe I was just intrigued by the fact that this much older man was falling for me. What had I gotten myself into?

I knew that Michael would be returning within the next week, so I had to cool things down with Xavier. I mean, there was no commitment between the two of us, but I didn't want anyone to get hurt. I told him that I thought things were going to fast, that we should slow things down a little. He and Michael were stationed in the same building, so he knew that Michael's company was coming back soon, and that was the reason for my backing down so suddenly.

He didn't put up a big fuss or anything.

He simply said, "When you are ready to stop playing games and settle down and want to be treated like a real woman is supposed to be treated, I'll be waiting for you."

My heart dropped. I was so disgusted with myself for doing the one thing to him that I never wanted to do. I hurt him really bad.

Visit 12

I was working as a cook today, so I was in the back. Ronnie called back and told me I had a visitor. I couldn't imagine who it was considering Michael wasn't due back for another week and I'd cooled things down with Xavier. I was wrong. There Michael was, right in my face, all smiles. I was kind of stunned and surprised all at once. Before I could say anything, he leaned over and planted a wet one on me. I was glad to see him and he me.

I left work early because I was so anxious to spend some time with him. Once we got back to my place, we couldn't keep our hands off each other. He took me right on the livingroom floor. I guess he must have really been horny, because he didn't even take the time to put a condom on. I guess in the heat of passion, I didn't ask him to. It was over so quick; it was almost as though nothing happened. He kissed me over and over again. I thought he would never stop. We both got cleaned up and put in a movie to watch.

We were sitting on the sofa watching the movie and someone knocked on the door. I wasn't expecting anyone, so I looked out the window. I saw Xavier's little red Fierro. I thought I'd died and gone straight to hell! There was another knock at the door. I froze. I mean, I couldn't move a muscle. Michael asked me if I was going to get the door. Eventually, I did. As soon as I opened it, Xavier just walked straight on in and sat down on the couch across from where Michael and I were sitting.

"What's up scrub?" he said to me.

"What's up man?" he said to Michael.

I couldn't believe what was happening. Finally I couldn't take it anymore, and I asked Xavier if he could step outside. He came. I'm sure this was real funny to him, but not the least bit funny to me.

"I knew you weren't any good. You want a brother when your ole man is gone, but you want to trip when he comes back. It looks like the jokes on you this time!"

He was right. I got busted. He laughed in my face, and then left. I know he was hurt by the way I did him, and I couldn't blame him for what he'd just done. It was kind of funny now that I think about it.

When I went back inside, I had a lot of explaining to do.

"Is that the way you were passing your time while I was away?" Michael asked.

We went back and forth for a little bit, and I apologized. I was feeling so guilty about what I'd done that I almost forgot to ask him how he managed to come back home a week early. Now the shoe was on the other foot! He started fumbling over his words and shit. Then he gave some lame excuse about his sister being sick, and Red Cross let him come home early for moral support. Yeah right! I guess I wasn't the only one with some skeletons in my closet. We called a truce and that was that.

Michael and I decided we were going to get an apartment and live together. We found a nice townhouse that was close to both of our jobs. It was nice being able to come home and be with my baby every night. We took turns preparing meals for each other. Some days when I didn't feel so well, he'd come home early from work and doctor on me. I didn't know what was wrong. I just kept getting sick, and I thought I had the flu or food poisoning. I ended up having to go to the emergency room because I passed out. They ran a bunch of tests, gave me an IV, and sent me home. The doctor made me a follow up appointment for one week.

Most of the time, I stayed in bed. That's just how awful I felt. Mama came over and brought me some soup she'd made. Of course, she had to preach to me about how I was living in sin. I didn't have the energy to argue with her, so she took advantage of the situation.

"Ain't nothing wrong with you but pregnant," she yelled.

Pregnant? I can't be, could I? Michael and I always used protection. Except the day he got back from where ever the hell he was. It had totally slipped my mind.

"Least you could do is protect yourself if you just have to fornicate," mama said. " With all them diseases going around, you gon end up with that AIDS stuff that's going around or whatever they call it!" she continued.

I ignored her once again. What was Michael going to think? How was he going to react? Should I tell him or just wait and see what the doctor says next week?

I followed up with the doctor, and mama was right (as usual). I was pregnant. I was pregnant with Michael's baby, I think. It had to be, because Xavier and I used protection. I didn't know what to do. I thought about having an abortion. That way no one had to know. If I did that, I may never be able to have children. I was losing my damn mind. That went against everything I believed in. I had to tell Michael, he deserved to know. He deserved to know that he was going to be a father.

I had to be sure that it was his baby. I left the doctor's office so fast once he confirmed my suspicions, I didn't even ask how far along he thought I was. I called him back and his calculations confirmed that it was Michael's baby. I conceived on the day he returned. The day we got so caught up in the heat of passion. The day we used our hormones instead of a condom.

Several days went by and I still hadn't decided what to do, so I called Ronnie. She had always been there for me and today was no different. I told her I was strongly considering getting an abortion. I knew how she felt about it since she had been trying, but to get pregnant but never could. I'd suggested that she and Ray, her husband of five years, go and see a fertility specialist. With the technology that we have nowadays, all you need is an egg and a sperm, and the doctors can do the rest.

"We are struggling to make ends meet as it is, there is no way we can afford to go and see a fertility specialist", she said.

"Besides, I think Ray's the one with the problem because I.... never mind."

She cut her sentence short as if she'd said something she wasn't meaning to say. That really got my attention. Me, being the curious person that I am, I just had to find out what she was about to say.

"Come on Ronnie, spit it out!" I shouted with anticipation.

"I ain't never told nobody this, but when I was sixteen years old, I got knocked up by this boy named Kool-Aid", she said.

Ronnie saw the expression on my face when she said that, so she began to explain.

"Well his name wasn't really Kool-Aid, that's just what everybody called him. His real name was Dexter."

"Anyway, he use to come around while mama was at work. He said that he wanted to protect me. One day, mama and me had a big argument about Kool-Aid and how much time we were spending together. She told me that she didn't want me seeing him anymore. Ofcourse, I did what I wanted to do.

I was at home alone all the time and I needed some companionship. As soon as mama went to work, Dexter came over, horny as hell! About two months later I found out I was pregnant. Needless to say, Dexter was no where to be found, and mama said that she wasn't raising any more babies. She took me to the Family Planning Clinic and made me get an abortion. I still haven't forgiven her to this day," she said with tears running down her face.

I couldn't believe what I'd just heard. I went over and gave my Ace-boon-coon a big hug. She needed it! She composed herself and spoke.

"That's why I think it's Ray with the problem."

I knew how she felt about abortions, but I also knew that she understood that whatever decisions I made, I felt, would be best for me and my situation. Either way, she would be there for me.

She offered to raise the baby as her own, but I couldn't do that. I didn't want the child to come up to me fifteen years later, angry with me because I gave it away. That would've been a total nightmare.

I made the appointment at the family planning clinic, and Ronnie was right there by my side. As we sat in the small, dull colored waiting room, I could tell she was uncomfortable. I couldn't blame her, I was as well, but I knew what had to be done.

After I completed all of the paperwork and returned it to the receptionist, the nurse led me into the examining room. It felt so cold in there. I changed into the gown she gave me, cracked the door as she instructed me to do, and went and sat down on the procedure table. The nurse came back into the room and began prepping me for the doctor. She put some cold blue jelly stuff on my stomach and turned the machine on. I noticed her positioning the monitor in a way that I couldn't see what was going on.

As she adjusted the speakers on the monitor, I heard a noise that sounded like a washing machine. I asked the nurse what it was, and she told me it was the fetal heart rate. The tears flooded my eyes. I asked if I could see, and although reluctant, the nurse agreed. Oh my God! It was my baby! That tiny little thing on the screen was my baby. She saw the pain I was in, so she quickly turned the monitor off, and exited the room to go and find the doctor.

I felt so empty and confused that I didn't know what to do. How could I possibly go through with this? How could I live with myself? Single women have been raising families for years, and besides, I didn't need a man to validate me, nor my ability to be a loving parent.

Before I realized it, I jumped down off the table and put my clothes back on. I was half way down the hall when I ran into the doctor, but I didn't stop. I burst through the doors leading to the waiting room so fast, I scared Ronnie half to death. I had to get out of there. I didn't have time to explain to her what was going on.

When we reached the parking lot, I started gasping for air. I didn't realize it, but I had been holding my breath for some time now, and I had finally released it. Ronnie reassured me that everything would be okay and that she would be there for me every step of the way, no matter what happened. I gave her a big hug and we left. Between the two of us, this day never happened.

When Michael got home, I told him I needed to talk with him. I didn't know how he was going to react, but he had a right to know that I was carrying his child. I think. As far as I was concerned, he was the father.

His response caught me off guard.

"You mean about our baby you're carrying?" with a huge smile on his face.

I couldn't believe it. He was actually happy that I was pregnant with his child. Just think, I wasn't even going to let him know about the baby.

He said "I do a count down on you every month, if you're a day late, I know it! I was just waiting on you to tell me!"

I was scared for nothing. He went on to tell me how he'd always wanted a family. He shared with me about how his ex-wife wouldn't give him any children, and how he hated that.

I know it may have been a little soon, but he started buying all sorts of baby stuff. We still had seven months to go. He'd hold my stomach and talk to our baby all the time. I think he was more excited about the pregnancy than I was. He already had names picked out. Ain't that something?

Michael was more concerned about the baby than he was about me. I couldn't eat any junk food, drink soda, or even sleep laying flat. He was really starting to get on my nerves. We had a huge argument, and I stomped out of the apartment. He ran behind me and grabbed my arm. I snatched away, but when I did this, I lost my balance and fell down the stairs. The next thing I remember, I was in the hospital with all sorts of tubes coming out of me. The doctor said there wasn't much he could do. My situation was basically touch and go. The trauma from the fall caused me to start having contractions, and my baby was not developed enough right then to survive birth. Mama had the preacher come and pray for me.

"The Lord takes care of babies and fools," he said.

The nurse came around every hour to check my vital signs. My blood pressure was too high, and my test results showed that my blood count was dropping fast. That meant that my baby was dead. Dead!

"This can't be happening to me! Everything I have loved in life has been taken away from me. Not my baby too!" I screamed over and over again.

Michael couldn't handle it; so he just walked out. He practically blamed me for losing the baby. All of this was my fault, according to him.

The doctor had to induce labor on me because I was too far along for a D&C. I had to give birth to a dead baby.

"Oh God! Please help me," I screamed until my throat refused to release any more cries.

When it was over, the doctor tried to take the baby away so I couldn't see it, but I wanted to. It was a little girl. She was an angel. I asked the nurse if she could take a picture of her, so I could have it. She was reluctant, but she did. I named her "Angel". I know she is in heaven with God right now.

Angela Weathered

Visit 13

It had been almost three months since the miscarriage. I totally secluded myself from the outside world. I wouldn't answer the telephone when it rang. My answering machine was so full of messages that I just turned it off.

Ronnie hadn't been around much either. Every time we were supposed to hook up, something would always "just come up" for her. We'd been friends much too long for me not to be concerned, so I gave her a call.

"I'm sorry...no one is home to....." Damn! That answering machine got on my nerves. I left a message anyway.

"Hey Ronnie, It's me, Neeka, give me a call girl, we need to talk." I hung up and that was it.

About one thirty in the morning, my telephone rang. This time I answered it. People only call that time of morning when it's important. It was Ronnie finally returning my call. I immediately jumped in on her case.

"Ronnie, you are my best friend in the world, yet I lost my baby, and you are the only one that hasn't called or anything. I want to know what's going on with you!" She didn't really have much to say.

"I—I'm sorry, OK! I have my own problems to deal with here, so forgive me if I can't hold your damn hand in everything you do!"

All I heard after that was the dial tone. I couldn't believe what had just happened. I must have been dreaming. After all that was my soul dog I was just talking to, not some stranger on the street. How could she have been so cold and insensitive to me of all people? At first I started to cry, then I got mad as hell. I wanted to know what was going on. I dialed the number again, and Ronnie's niece, Tabetha, answered the telephone. "Hey auntie Neeka, I'll go get aunt Ronnie," she said.

While I was waiting for Ronnie to come to the telephone, I heard a man's voice. My man's voice! I swear that voice sounded just like Michael. It couldn't be him. He didn't have any reason to be at Ronnie's house, especially not at that hour of the night. Just then, someone picked up the telephone but they didn't say anything. I knew someone was on the phone because you could hear them breathing.

"Ronnie, is that you?" I asked, but didn't get an answer.

"What's going on over there?" Still, no answer.

I got the dial tone again. Something just wasn't right. I got dressed, grabbed my keys and headed out the door. I had to find out what was going on.

When I arrived, I knocked on the door, which was slightly opened. Ronnie was sitting on the couch with a bottle of Alize` in her hands. Her body was shaking uncontrollably.

"I knew you would come," she said in a slurred voice. Her eyes were almost swollen shut because she'd been crying so much. Ronnie knew damn well that she couldn't hold her liquor. I don't know why she even tried to drink.

She sat there and sobbed. I went over to her to comfort her, putting my problems on the back burner. As I held her in my arms like my granny used to do me, she cried like there was no tomorrow. I'd never seen her like that before. I'd never seen anyone like that before. For the longest time, we didn't say a word.

Finally, after what seemed like forever, she spoke. "I'm sorry Neeka, I never meant to take out my frustrations on you. I should have been there for you, instead I was hurting you more".

I didn't know what to say because I didn't know what she was talking about. I had a sickening feeling growing in the pit of my stomach. I had to get up and start moving around to get my blood circulating again.

As I walked to the other side of the room, I noticed a brown wallet on the floor by the couch. It looked like the same wallet I bought Michael for his birthday. I walked over and kicked it under the couch with my foot. Ronnie was so busy crying that she didn't notice what I had done.

I had to find out if that was, indeed, Michael's wallet, but I couldn't do it with Ronnie sitting there. I suggested that she go and take a shower to settle down. After she left the room and I heard the shower running, I went back over to the couch and retrieved the wallet. When I picked it up and looked at it closely, my suspicions were confirmed. It was Michael's wallet. My whole world came tumbling down. I opened the wallet and saw me and Michael's smiling faces on a picture we'd taken a couple of months before this mess.

I couldn't have timed it better. Just as I sat down to go through his wallet some more, I heard someone at the door fumbling with keys. It sounded like they didn't know which one to use.

"Open the door Ronnie, my key won't work!" he yelled. It was Michael!

I looked around the room trying to find some place to hide because I didn't want him to see me. I found the coat closet on the other side of the living room, and jumped in it. Just as I closed the door, Michael came walking through the front door. I could see him through the louvers in the door, but he couldn't see me. We had the nerve to be wearing the clothes that I bought him to some other woman's house. That scrub!

He took his jacket off, and came over to hang it up in the closet that I was hiding in. Just as he placed his hand on the doorknob, Ronnie came into the room with nothing on but a too little towel wrapped around her.

"What the hell are you doing back here!" she screamed at him while, all the time, looking around to see if I'd left.

The only thing that I'd brought with me were my keys, so I didn't have to grab anything before I rushed into the closet.

Michael finally got up enough courage to speak. "Look Ronnie, I'm sorry! I realize I got a little carried away earlier, but you got to admit, I wasn't looking for you to get pregnant and shit! I thought you said you were using protection, now you gone tell me you pregnant with my baby? How was I supposed to react?"

I know I couldn't have heard him right. I know my man didn't just say that he'd gotten my best friend, my married best friend, pregnant. I know my ears were just deceiving me. Before I had time to absorb what he'd just said, I found myself leaping out of the closet with a baseball bat in my hands, swinging at any and everything that got into my way.

When all of my energy was gone, I fell to the floor. It felt as though my soul had been instantly ripped from my body. The two people that I cared about more that anyone or anything in this world had betrayed me in the worst possible way. My whole life passed before my eyes.

Ronnie crawled over to me on the floor. She had blood coming from her mouth. Her skin was so light that you could see the bruises already. I couldn't believe that I'd done that to her, but she deserved it! I looked around trying to find Michael. He was out cold with his back against the wall. That bastard!

"I'm sorry Neeka, I never meant for this to happen.....it just did," said Ronnie as though her words were some kind of consolation to me. "I never meant for things to go this far. It was all a big mistake!"

I came right back at her. " Was it a mistake only because I found out about it?" being as sarcastic as I possibly could be.

"You know I've been having problems at home. Michael came over looking for you and he saw how upset I was. He began to comfort me, and well, one thing led to another," she said with those fake ass tears rolling down her face.

She could cry a river on command. I wanted to reach out and slap her, but I couldn't bring myself to do it. I grabbed my keys and left. With friends and lovers like those two, I didn't need any enemies. Michael still lay stiff on the floor as I walked out.

Angela Weathered

Visit 14

On my ride home, I cried like there was no tomorrow. At that moment, it seemed as though there wasn't going to be one. I had to pull my car over to the side of the road and pull myself together. As I wiped my eyes, I noticed car lights coming closer. They were beginning to blind me, so I put my hands up to shield the light. Who ever it was finally turned the lights off, got out of their car, and started walking towards me. My eyes were so swollen, I could hardly see. Finally, as he got closer, I could see that it was Eric.

"I thought that was you driving all crazy, what's going on?" he asked being his usual curious self.

I wasn't in the mood for no damn games tonight. I guess he realized that when I looked up at him because he saw that I had been crying.

Eric reached in and opened my car door. He got down on his knees and pulled me close to him and told me that everything was going to be all right. Being in his arms, at that moment, made me feel that I could trust his words. Regardless of his shortcomings, I knew that Eric was a man of his word, and that he wanted only what was best for me.

He offered to drive me home, and come and pick my car up in the morning. He locked all of my doors and led me to his car.

I didn't feel like being alone that night, so Eric took me to his place. When we got there, he saw that I was a mess, so he gave me a pair of his sweats to put on and he ran me some bath water. Why did he have to be such a mama's boy? I asked myself this question once again.

After I removed my clothes and eased into the warm bubble bath, I heard a knock at the door. He came in with a glass of wine and some lit scented candles that he placed on the counter top and around the bathtub. I could hear the soft sounds of jazz coming from the CD player in the living room. He always was romantic. He offered to get me something to eat, but after all of the excitement, I didn't have much of an appetite. After handing me the glass of wine, he left and closed the door behind him. I laid back, closed my eyes and sipped on the wine.

I must have fallen asleep, because when I opened my eyes, the bath water was ice cold, and the candles had burned almost all the way down. I grabbed the towel and dried off. I looked around for the sweats, but they weren't in the bathroom. I wrapped the towel around me and headed up the hall.

I went into the bedroom first. Fresh linen had been put on the bed and the covers were turned back. There was no sign of Eric. I could still smell the Nautica Scented candles that had burned out only moments ago. The ceiling fan was on low and you could see the blade's reflection against the wall as the moonlight filtered through the blinds.

I walked up the hallway back into the living room. Eric was sound asleep on the sofa with an empty wineglass on the floor next to him. The CD player was still putting out some smooth sounds. You know the kind that brings lovers so much intimacy and passion. He looked like a newborn baby, lying there sound asleep. I bent over to kiss him on his forehead, but when my lips touched his skin, I felt the need to linger there for a moment. I kissed him again, first on his eyes, then on his pink lips. As my tongue slowly parted his lips, I could feel him coming to life. He began to reciprocate my passion. I let my towel fall to the floor as I climbed on top of him, straddling him with my naked body. His breathing intensified.

I know that he still had very strong morals when it came to premarital sex, but right then and there, we felt so right together. The look on his face said one thing, but his sex organ was saying another.

"If two people care for each other, can't that be enough?" I said to him.

I really wanted him. He was the one I really wanted to loose my virginity to so many years ago. He hesitated for a moment, and then he raised me up off of him and headed down the hallway towards the bedroom. I went behind him apologizing for not respecting his wishes. I felt horrible. He didn't say a word. He just kept on walking until he reached the dresser in his bedroom.

I stood behind him as he searched through his things. After a moment, he closed the drawer and turned to face me.

"I think you are right, we do care for each other. I have loved you from the first day we met, and I should share my special moment with someone I truly love. The only woman I've ever loved!"

He opened his hand and revealed the gold wrapped condom that he'd gotten out of his drawer.

"I've been saving this for a special occasion, and I can't find one more special than this," he said.

We began to kiss passionately until I felt his manhood start to rise and press against my flesh. I was already butt-naked, so he began to peel off his clothes as well. We laid back onto his bed and kissed, sucked, and nibbled on each other in places you can only imagine. I felt his anticipation growing stronger and stronger, so I removed the condom from it's foil package and placed it on his stiff penis, wanting to wait no more to receive him inside of me.

He moved so slow and cautiously as if I was the virgin and he didn't want to hurt me. He caressed my breasts over and over again. I would feel the dampness grow between my legs more and more. I pulled him on top of me and parted my legs for him to enter my warmth. With slow, rhythmic strokes, he quickly came. His body shuttered from head to toe. Although it was over so quickly, I didn't mind. I knew it would come fast for him because it was his first time experiencing the depths of a woman. He made love to me long before he penetrated my body.

"If I knew it felt that good, I wouldn't have waited so long," he said jokingly.

That night, we made love three more times, each time being more intense that the one before. Each time, he made me feel things I'd never felt before. Our bodies clicked. Regardless of the experience all my past lovers had, none of them took me to the places Eric had that night. I laid in his warm arms and drifted off to sleep.

I arrived home about eight-thirty that morning, still exhausted from the wild night before. As I looked at myself in the mirror, I saw a new me. I wasn't that self-pitying person that I was the day before. I'd reclaimed my self-worth. I was moving forward from that moment on.

As I got closer to the mirror, I noticed that I was still wearing Eric's gray sweat suit, and the memories of just a few hours ago flooded my head. I had to cool myself down, so I turned on the shower and, without letting it warm up, jumped right in. I closed my eyes and stood there for a moment.

As I began to dry myself off, there was a knock at the door. I didn't know who it could possibly have been at that time of the morning, after all, it was Saturday. Before I could get to the door, there was another knock.

"Hold the hell on!" I yelled, starting to get real pissed off. I swung the door open, and there was this Roger-from-What's Happening looking police officer standing there.

"Is there something I can help you with officer?"

I quickly looked at his nametag and kicked into my flirtatious mode; he didn't seem to take the bait, but that's O.K. Besides, he was too ugly.

Love Don't Live Here Anymore

"Are you Ms. Shaneeka Spencer?" he asked.

"Well, that depends on what you're here for," I replied, batting my eyes and smiling at him.

"Look Miss, I'm not here to play games! Now, are you Shaneeka Spencer?" he shouted.

He was getting really irritated with me by then. He was so nerdy that he wouldn't realize a fine woman if one slapped him in his face!

"Yes, I'm Shaneeka Spencer, why?" He had me curious now.

He started in. "Ms. Spencer, you are under arrest for the attempted murder of one Mr. Michael Washington. You have the right to remain silent.... And so on....do you understand these rights as I have read them to you?" He said with a smirk on his face.

"This must be some kind of joke right?" I asked him as he began to handcuff me.

"I want to call my lawyer!" I yelled knowing good and damn well I didn't have one. Who was I kidding?

He slapped the handcuffs on my wrists and smiled.

"Afraid not Miss Thang!" That was the first sign of that dufus having any real human qualities. All of my neighbors were standing around outside of my apartment building being noisy as he led me to his squad car.

"I knew that tramp was crazy!" someone yelled.

"Yeah, she ain't nothing but a whore anyway, I'm glad to see her leaving!" another person shouted.

Ouch! That stung. Did my neighbors really think of me like that? Was I really that bad of a person as they were making me out to be?

When we got down to the police station, they finger printed me, took my picture, and threw me into a holding cell with three other women. I heard a lot of horror stories about what happens to the new piece of meat when you go on lock-down, and I wasn't about to become another statistic.

"What's your problem!" I yelled at the lady with the pleather (play leather) red mini-skirt on. She quickly turned away from me.

That wasn't so bad I thought to myself. I went over and sat down on the bench.

"Ms. Spencer, come with me," a female officer said. She took me to a small room and made me undress.

"What the hell do you think you are doing to me?" I asked her as she started touching me.

"This is only procedure ma'am, now drop'em!" she yelled, showing me that she wasn't intimidated by my attitude.

I did as I was told. Before escorting me to my cell, she gave me an orange pair of coveralls, the Standard County Prison Uniform, to put on. I felt so humiliated.

In the cell, there was a small cot with dingy sheets, a sink that was rusted, and a toilet that needed a good cleaning. That place was disgusting! I had to get out of there and fast!

I laid down on the cot and closed my eyes. I was exhausted. My ears started ringing out the words that Ronnie had uttered to Michael "I'm having your baby...I'm having your baby," over and over again. I saw myself jumping out of the closet with the bat in my hand, but then my mind went blank, and before I realized it, I was sound asleep.

I was awakened by the sound of the police stick being raked across the bars on the cell.

"Come with me, you have a visitor," said the lady police officer. I knew it could only be one person, Ronnie, and she was the last person I wanted to see. She was the only other person that knew about what happened last night. I was wrong, it was Eric. He stopped by my apartment on his way to work to see how I was doing, and my neighbor told him what happened and how the police had carried me away in handcuffs. For once having a noisy neighbor was a good thing.

He told me that he was going to post my bail after I went before the judge that afternoon. He'd spoken with Attorney Joseph Farley, and explained to him what happened, and paid him a retainer fee.

"Everything is going to be okay, trust me," he said.

I didn't doubt him one bit.

Mr. Farley went before the judge and pleaded my case for me. He used temporary insanity as my defense.

"Your Honor, as you will learn, my client has be an upstanding and contributing citizen in her community. She has no prior record and deeply regrets the events that have taken place. The defendant has recently suffered a great loss, one which was caused, in part, due to the Plaintiff's negligence."

He went on. "During her grieving period, the Defendant, Ms. Spencer, walked in on her best friend of five years, telling Ms. Spencer's estranged lover, the plaintiff, Mr. Michael Washington, that she was pregnant with his child. Ms. Spencer, admittedly, snapped."

Mr. Farley looked back at me and continued.

"So I beg of you, Your Honor, to consider these facts when making your judgment. Thank you."

Michael's attorney got up and tried to make him seem like the only victim, but the judge saw right through him. I was really impressed with Mr. Farley, and apparently, the judge was too. He let me off with time served, two years probation, and court ordered therapy to help me deal with everything that had happened.

Angela Weathered

Visit 15

Eric didn't want me being alone, so he suggested that I move in with him for a while. We stopped by my place so I could grab a few things, and we made our way over to his place. He wanted to, once again, share his life and his home with me. This time, he came to me correct.

"Shaneeka, I lost you one time because I didn't stand up and do the right thing, I don't want to lose you again. Will you marry me?"

Don't ask me why I hesitated to answer him. It wasn't because I didn't love him, because I did. My love for him had become more evident to me in those last few days than it ever had. I just didn't want to say yes out of obligation. He'd done so much for me during this time than anyone had ever done for me before. I owed him more than just my hand in marriage.

"I know things have been moving kind of fast, but after all that we've been through, we always end up together. We've already wasted too much time as it is," he said as serious as a heart attack.

"Shhh! You don't have to say any more," I told him.

"Yes, I'll marry you! I'll be Mrs. Eric Johnson!"

After I accepted Eric's proposal, we decided that I would move into his place since it was larger; besides, just about all of my stuff was over there already. I only had two more months left on my lease, so I bought it out. I gave my thirty-day notice, and paid one months rent.

Eric, being the bachelor that he was, didn't have much food in the house, so before he left for work, he wrote me a note with a crisp hundred-dollar bill attached to it saying:

"Go get some food baby, cause you know I like some meat on those bones of yours" Love Eric.

Sometimes he was so corny. In a good way that is. I wouldn't have traded him for the world.

I had the day off, so I straightened up a little before going to the store. I looked around at our apartment and yelled "Home sweet Home!" For the first time in my life I felt what it meant to be loved and have a place I could truly call home. I jumped up and down, turning around in a circle like a kid on Christmas Day. This place felt so good. I added a woman's touch to warm the house up a little bit. A couple of flowers here, a few pictures there and a lot of love everywhere. I picked up the picture of Eric and me, and I kissed it softly.

As I sat there, I thought about the last conversation that I'd had with Marcus about our getting married and all. I wanted to call him and let him know about my wedding plans with Eric. That was the least I could do. I owed him that much. He'd always treated me with nothing but kindness the whole time I'd known him. I wanted him to be a part of my special day.

"It will be a little awkward for me, but if he makes you happy, then I am happy for you. I don't think I'll be able to make it to the ceremony, though, because I will be taking midterms. I promise, I'll try my best to be there for you Neeka."

I couldn't ask for anything more than that from him. Marcus was truly one of a kind.

I was about to leave for the store when the telephone rang. I started to let the answering machine pick it up, but I went on and answered.

"Hello!" I said.

"Hey Neeka, I really need to talk to you!"

I recognized the voice right away and wished a thousand times over that I'd let the machine pick up. It was Michael. I hadn't spoken to him in almost three months, and when I had, I was in court fighting for my freedom because of him. I didn't have anything to discuss with him. He didn't realize it, but by calling, he'd just opened up a can of whoop-ass and I was about to go off on him.

"You are crazier than I thought you were. You have some nerve calling here talking about you need to talk to me. You don't have a damn thing I want to hear! First of all, your sorry ass put me through hell and made me lose my baby. Then you walk out of my life and into my so-called best friend's bed and get her pregnant. You think we have something to discuss? You really are crazy!"

I gave him the dial tone with quickness. It felt good too. A few seconds later the telephone rang again. This time, I did let the machine pick up. For some reason, I stood there and listened to him go on and say whatever it was he felt he had to say.

"I can't live without you Neeka. I need ....beeeeppppp."

The answering machine cut off before he had a chance to finish his sentence. The telephone rang again.

"Neeka, I need you in my life. Ronnie didn't mean shit to me. You have to believe that! You have to give me another chance!"

He was crying by that time. That served his ass right. I had to give him another chance, yeah right! I started to pick up the telephone and tell him that all I have to do is stay black and die, but that might have been too complicated for him to understand. I made myself a mental noted and called the telephone company and have my number changed when I get back from the grocery store.

This must have been Pick-On-Shaneeka day because when I finally made it to the store, Ronnie was there shopping, her big belly and all. I started to turn around and leave, but I figured I couldn't run forever. I needed to face her once and for all to clear the air.

She saw me immediately and came running over to me.

"I wanted to call you Neeka, but I figured that I'd be the last person on earth you would want to talk to. I can't say that I'd blame you after what I did though."

She went on. "I just wanted to let you know that it's over between me and Michael. It never should have happened."

I couldn't believe that she was standing there telling me that mess. She had some nerve! Like them breaking up was going to make everything all right.

"You stand here, with a stomach full with my boyfriend's... excuse me, ex-boyfriend's baby, telling me that everything is over? I don't think so!" I said, getting my can of whoop-ass out again. I was on a roll now, so I continued.

"And another thing, you called yourself my best friend while all along you were having yourself a good time screwing my man, while I was laying in the hospital losing my baby? I will never forgive you for that! You will rot in hell first!" I walked away. I was so upset, I left the store without buying a thing.

I headed back home, stopping off at Mickey D's on the way. When I arrived home, I went over to the answering machine to check for any new messages. They were all from Michael. I immediately called Bell South and had my number changed and unlisted.

Visit 16

The morning of my wedding, the telephone rang. I didn't feel like talking to anyone because I didn't want anything to ruin my special day. After the fourth ring, I finally looked at the caller ID. It was Eric's mother.

"I don't need her shit today! I screamed out loud. The telephone was now on it's sixth ring. Why hadn't the stupid answering machine picked up yet? I was certain that she wasn't calling for me. Our relationship was still far from being civil, even though I would soon be her daughter-in-law. After eight rings, she must have realized that no one was home and hung up.

I had the place to myself. Eric stayed the night at his cousin's house last night because I was very superstitious about him seeing me before the wedding ceremony. I sat at the end of my bed and thought back on everything that had happened over the course of my life. All of the Michael's, Cedrick's, and Tyreek's were gone for good. I didn't have to worry about the guilt of Mr. Leroy touching me anymore. I was safe now. I would be with someone who would love me for me and not because of what I could give him. I was finally experiencing what true love was really all about.

The telephone rang again and broke my train of thought.

"Damn! I screamed as I looked at the caller ID.

It was Eric's mother again. I didn't know why she kept on calling. She knew that Eric was not home. What was so urgent that she had to keep calling? It must have been important because she just kept calling. I finally answered.

"Hello!"

"Hello Shaneeka, how are you today?" She asked as if she really wanted to know.

"I'm fine Mrs. Johnson," I said, trying real hard to be polite. After all, she was my elder. It was so hard. Just hearing her voice made me cringe. She was just plain evil! I knew that I didn't have to like her, but I would try to get along with her for Eric's sake. I owed him that much. Besides, he knew his mother was a B-I-T-C-H.!

"I know that you are wondering why I'm calling," she said. That was a very true statement. She'd never had anything positive to say to me. What could she possibly want with me now, especially on my wedding day.

"As a matter of fact, I was wondering about that," I responded before I even knew it. She disregarded my comment and went on.

"I know that today is going to be a very special day for you and my son. I just wanted to call and wish you all the best and to let you know that I love both of you. Regardless of what you may think, I am glad that you are going to be my daughter-in-law."

Now that was the last thing I was expecting her to say. I was speechless! This was too good to be true! Were my ears deceiving me? I didn't stop her to find out. She just kept right on talking. It was almost as like if she had stopped talking, she would have lost her courage, so she continued without taking a breath.

"I know that I haven't been the easiest person in the world to get along with." Boy, what an understatement I thought.

"I may have said some things that were out of order, but I never doubted one minute that you were good for Eric. I was just so afraid that I would lose my only child forever. I was afraid that he wouldn't have time for his mama anymore. It's hard being alone. To have

Love Don't Live Here Anymore

everything you love taken away from you, leaving you with nothing."

I had to cut in.

"I do understand what you are saying, Mrs. Johnson. I know exactly what you mean. I want you to understand something, though, I am not out to steal your son away from you. We love each other very much. I also know that he loves you very much as well. I would be a fool to try and take that away from him. I wouldn't even try to. Besides, Eric's heart is so big, he has enough room in it for the both of us to share," I said almost blushing.

"I'm glad we had a chance to talk, Shaneeka, and get all of this out in the open. You know what I mean?"

"Yes, I know what you mean, Ms. J."

"Good, because I really do want my son to be happy, and that means having you in his life. I couldn't have asked for a better daughter-in-law", she said.

"Thank you, Mrs. Johnson."

"You're welcome Shaneeka. Oh, and one more thing," she said.

"Yes, Mrs. Johnson?"

"From now on, call me mama, okay baby."

"Very well mama, I will see you later on today."

After we hung up, I began to cry. This time, they were tears of joy. I was simply overwhelmed. My wedding day would be perfect after all.

Eric and I decided on a small, intimate wedding ceremony downtown on the River, just above the river's bank. Just as the sun was going down, we'd exchange our wedding vows. All of our guests held lit candles to add to the ambiance. It was so perfect.

My wedding gown was made of ivory bridal satin. I mean really, there was no reason to pretend like I was still a virgin by wearing a snow-white gown. Eric knew he wasn't the only man that had entered my special zone, but he would be the only one to ever go there again after today.

My gown had a ten-foot cathedral train on it. When mama and me first walked into the bridal boutique, this

101

dress was the first one we saw. It was perfect. I would have loved to wear mama's wedding dress, but she said her marriage to daddy had caused her so much pain, she didn't want to jinx mine in any way. I had to respect her wishes. Despite all of their marriage difficulties, he was still my daddy and I wanted him to be a part of my life again. I wanted to walk down the isle on his arm.

As I walked down the flowered path, all eyes were on me. I was the spotlight. Just as I reached the end of the walkway, I noticed Eric standing there. Tears instantly dropped from my eyes. He winked at me and blew me a kiss. The live band played soft music as I made my way down to join my soul mate for an eternity. When I got closer to Eric, his mouth flew open. You could see the amazement all over his face as he waited for me to take my place next to him. We would begin our new life together as one.

After the wedding reception, Eric and I went back to the Ritz Carlton where we were staying until we left for our honeymoon. We'd fly out first thing that next morning to our honeymoon location, which was undisclosed to me.

The room was decorated perfectly. The bar was stocked with the finest champagne available. There was a large bowl filled with grapes, cheese, strawberries, and crackers of all kinds. There was a can of whipped cream in the refrigerator.

Eric picked me up and carried me over the threshold, straight into the bedroom. He eased me down onto the bed, and went into the bathroom. When he came back out, he proceeded to remove my clothes. He kissed my shoulders, neck and then my lips. I began to remove his remaining clothes. His soldier was already standing at attention. I began to massage it gently.

"Not yet," he said.

He grabbed me by the hand and led me into the bathroom. There were scented candles lit throughout the bathroom. The lights had been dimmed, and the jacuzzi jets hummed softly.

We both climbed into the warm bubble bath and held each other close. He caressed my body, and I did the same to him. My breasts began to swell from anticipation as his tongue glided gently around them. He placed his hands under my butt and slowly lifted me out of the water, onto the edge of the bathtub with my legs spread apart.

The warmth of his tongue felt so good as he made tiny circles around my tiny, swollen jewel. My heart began to race a hundred miles per hour. I could literally feel it beating outside of my chest. As I reached my orgasm, my body shook uncontrollably. I wanted to make him feel as good as he made me feel. I grabbed his arm and pulled him up next to me. I began to lick his tiny nipples, down to his stomach, until finally placing his manhood deep into my awaiting mouth, taking in his entire length. He grabbed the back of my head, moving it in a slow circular motion. The moans of pleasure coming deep from within his throat really turned me on.

"I've never had this done to me. It feels so damn good!" he said with a big smile on his face.

I knew that I was taking him to a foreign place, but I wanted to show him all that love had to offer both of us. I began to work him faster and harder until I felt his love juices explode from within. He let out a loud scream.

"Oh God, yes!" he said.

I smiled knowing that I'd just given my husband the ultimate orgasm. That was only just the beginning. We climbed out of the bathtub and into the bed, still soaking wet. There was kissing and caressing that night. It wasn't long before Eric was ready to go at it again. He entered me gently, and took long, slow strokes. Within seconds, we were both reaching a simultaneous orgasm.

The next morning we left for our honeymoon. The Cayman Islands. We were there for two weeks, and I was definitely in Paradise.

Angela Weathered

Visit 17

When we got back from our honeymoon, we were exhausted. Eric wasn't supposed to go back to work for another three days, but when he listened to the message his supervisor left, he went to work early. He was trying to get a promotion, and felt that if he showed how dedicated he was, it would help him out. Dedication was one of his finer qualities. He went back to work the morning after we got back. That left me with nothing to do, so I decided to go shopping.

"Hey Neeka!" I heard a voice say as soon as I walked into the store.

"Damn!" I said to myself.

It was Ronnie. I could tell her squeaky voice anywhere. She wobbled over to me

"Hey Ronnie," I yelled back trying to be cordial.

I figured we might as well talk and get everything out into the open.

"You want to join me for a bite to eat?" I asked. She seemed surprised that I was being nice to her after all she'd done to me. I guess a guilty conscience will do that to you. We grabbed a booth in WD Crowley's. I ordered sirloin tips with a baked potato. She ordered a cheeseburger and french fries.

"You know you should really try to eat a little more healthy being pregnant and all. By the way, when is the baby due?" I asked, surprising myself.

"In two weeks....look Shaneeka, (I knew she was getting serious on me because that's the only time she ever called me by my real name) we need to talk about this. I need to explain to you what happened. I owe you atleast that much."

I shook my head signaling her to go on. We needed to get past this point. She went on. "I would do anything to take back the pain that I caused you, but I can't. I miss having you in my life. It's like a part of me is missing. I love you, Neeka. You're like the sister I never had." She looked away as her eyes filled with tears, but she continued to talk.

"Ray hadn't been home in almost a week, and when he did show up, it was to tell me that he wanted a divorce from me, and that he had somebody else. I was devastated! He told me that he didn't love me anymore, and hadn't loved me for quite some time. Then, he walked into the bedroom, grabbed all the clothes he could carry, and left. He walked out of my life for good."

I understood the pain she must have felt, but why would she turn around and cause me the same pain? It just didn't make sense to me.

"I grabbed the bottle of Alize` from the refrigerator and drunk the whole thing. You know I don't drink! I got tore up! I was passed out on the couch when I heard a knock at the door. I thought it was Ray coming back to tell me that he really didn't mean the things he said and that he did want to work things out. It wasn't Ray, it was Michael and he was drunk as hell. He told me that he had been trying to get in contact with you for the longest, but that you wouldn't return any of his telephone calls or pages. When he finally got your telephone number off of his mama's caller ID, you changed it. He fell to his knees right in front of me and started crying. When I went over to him to comfort him, one thing led to another and I ended up pregnant. I promise you Neeka, it had only happened once. I promise!"

I needed a few minutes to digest what she'd just told me. I knew that Ronnie was telling the truth, but it still hurt like hell. By the time she finished telling her story, I was crying too. Michael walked out on her and the baby just like he'd done to me.

"I'm not going to lie, Ronnie, it's going to be hard to get back the trust that I had in you, but you are still my Ace-boon-coon and ain't no man gonna change that." I said, letting her know that I did still love her too. We gave each other a big hug, and started back in on our food that was now ice cold.

The waitress walked up to refill our drinks just as we were ending our 'crying session'. So much tension had been released from both of us. It felt good. Me and my girl were partners again.

When I reached for my glass of tea, Ronnie noticed my wedding ring. I was a little embarrassed.

"I just wanted to let you know that your wedding ceremony was beautiful." Ronnie said smiling because she knew I didn't know that she was there.

That caught me off guard because I hadn't invited her. I know that she saw the disappointment in my eyes. There was no doubt that she would have been a major part of my special day if everything hadn't been so messed up.

"I was standing in the very back. I guess since it was kind of dark, you couldn't see me. Besides, I didn't want to ruin your wedding. I just wanted to be there for you," she said, answering the puzzled look on my face.

When we finished eating, Ronnie reached into her handbag and pulled out a large gold envelope.

"I was going to mail this to you today, but since you are here, I can give it to you in person," she said as she handed it to me.

"What is this?"

"I won't say, but put it somewhere safe and don't open it unless something happens to me, OK?"

"Why are you talking like that Ronnie, you know ain't nothing gonna happen to you!"

"Well I hope not, but just in case, take this. Ray has been saying some crazy shit to me since he found out that I'm pregnant by Mich....somebody else, and I don't trust him. Please promise me this, Neeka." You could see the embarrassment on her face when she made that statement. She handed me the envelope, gave me another hug, and walked away. She didn't even say goodbye.

Love Don't Live Here Anymore

Visit 18

At two-thirty in the morning, my telephone rang. I got that sick feeling in the pit of my stomach all over again. The same feeling I got when my grandfather died.

"This is Dr. Carter from the Medical Center, may I speak with Ms. Shaneeka Spencer?"

"This is she, is something wrong?" By this time I was scared to death. Not answering my question, he went on.

"As I said earlier, I'm Dr. Carter, Ronnie is my patient. Ms. Spencer, there has been an accident, and she's in critical condition."

"Oh my God!" I yelled which woke Eric up.

"Ronnie listed you as her only emergency contact in her medical records, so that's why I'm calling you. Ms. Spencer, Ronnie was injured real bad, and it doesn't look good. It doesn't look good. You may want to come down here as soon as possible!"

"Oh my God, Ronnie is dying!" I yelled, immediately dropping the telephone. I grabbed my clothes that I'd worn that day and quickly got dressed. By the time I was fully dressed, Eric had on his jeans and a pair of loafers. When I headed out the door, he grabbed his shirt and ran after me.

"You are in no shape to drive, Shaneeka," he said, grabbing the keys out of my hand. I didn't argue with him because I knew he was right. I was petrified. I'd seen her only hours ago and now she lay dying in the hospital. Eric was doing sixty-five mph down Buena

Vista Rd. That was thirty-five mph over the posted speed limit.

We were flying down the road when, out of nowhere, this red sports car came flying towards us. A police car was right behind it. The car seemed to being coming towards us head-on. Eric swerved to miss the car, but it was too late. The car hit us, causing our car to hydroplane and slam into a telephone pole.

I looked over to see if Eric was OK, but I couldn't see him because the car was filled with smoke. The car was on fire underneath the hood, so I had to hurry up and get out of there. I climbed out of my window as quickly as I could. I was in excruciating pain. The dashboard had crushed both of my legs.

I crawled around to the driver's side of the car and tried to open Eric's door, but it was stuck. By that time, the police officer had backup and was able to come over and help me. He picked me up and carried me to the other side of the street. Afterwards, he ran back over and tried to rescue Eric. He tried to open the door, but couldn't. He had to use his police stick to break the window. He reached in and got the door open. Eric was pinned under the steering wheel, but the officer fault with all of his might to get him out. Finally, he succeeded. I had to sit there and watch him struggle to free my husband from the burning car, because I couldn't move my legs.

Once the officer had Eric out of the car, he picked him up and ran as quickly as he could across the street with him. The car exploded seconds later. The ambulance finally arrived. There were three paramedics. One of them came to care for me, while the other two went to see about Eric. One of them kneeled down to check Eric's pulse, but seconds later, stood up again, shaking his head.

"Is my husband going to be OK?" I asked, knowing that he was gone.

I tried to get up and go to him, but my legs just wouldn't work. I saw another police car pull up and transport the suspect to the station. The officer went to get the handcuffed suspect and transfer him to the other waiting police car. When I looked up, I saw that the person in handcuffs was none other than Ray, Ronnie's estranged husband! I fainted.

When I woke up, I was in the emergency room with all kinds of tubes running through my body. The doctor had given me a sedative to help me relax, so I didn't know if I was coming or going. My husband was dead, and my best friend lay dying. There wasn't a damn thing I could do for either one of them. I wanted the doctor to give me something to make me sleep. That way, I wouldn't have to deal with all of the tragedy going on around me.

The doctor explained to me that both of my legs were broken, one of my kidneys were severely bruised, and I had a couple of broken ribs. He said that with time and physical therapy, all of my wounds would heal. Including my broken heart.

After three days of being in the hospital, I had to get out of that room. The walls were closing in on me, and I was beginning to suffocate. I asked the nurse to push me downstairs to see Ronnie. At first, she was reluctant, but I convinced her that it would be good for me. She finally agreed.

Ronnie had been shot in the head apparently by Ray. That's why the cops were chasing him. A neighbor heard gunshots from their apartment, and called the police. When she heard the shots, she went out into the breezeway to see what was going on. That's when she saw Ray running out of the apartment. She quickly ran inside only to find Ronnie lying on the floor, face down, with blood coming from her head.

Ronnie was lying there so lifeless. All of her color was gone. Her beautiful face had been battered. Her eyes were swollen shut, and her lips were busted. My heart sank seeing her like that. I couldn't hold back the tears. Before I realized anything, I'd reached over and grabbed her hand. She didn't respond.

"You better wake up girl, you know that baby gone be here soon," I said, wishing she would open her eyes and look at me.

"When I leave here, the first thing I'm going to do is go and get you some make up and fix your hair. You know you ain't supposed to be out in public looking like that! The SBG Crew has an image to uphold, and you aren't doing your part right now" I said as I started crying again.

"I can't make it without you, Veronica Alexandria Foster! Now wake up!" I screamed. All of a sudden, I felt her squeeze my hand as if she was trying to tell me something. A tear ran down her battered face. I didn't wipe it.

The alarms on the machine went off. I grabbed the emergency call button and started yelling.

"Somebody, anybody, please help!" I screamed at the top of my lungs. The doctors burst through the doors and were running toward the bed that Ronnie was laying in. The nurse that brought me down to see Ronnie had returned and quickly rolled me out of the room. I heard the machine flat-line. I knew that Ronnie was gone.

On the way back upstairs, I asked the nurse to take me to the chapel. When I got there, there was only one other person in the tiny room. He was kneeling at the altar praying. I went to the front and lit two candles. One for my beloved husband, Eric, and one for my dear friend, Ronnie. I began to pray; something I hadn't done in a long time.

"Heavenly Father, I know that I have done a lot of things wrong lately, but I also know that you are a forgiving God. I am asking..... no, I am begging of you, right now, to work this thing out. I don't know how much more my broken heart can bare. It was your will to take Eric. I don't understand why right now, but I know that you have all knowledge. If it is your will to take Ronnie, then I know you must do that also, but please God, don't take everything or everybody that I've ever loved from me. I will always cherish the wonderful times that you

allowed me to share with the both of them. For that, I am grateful. I know that Eric is looking down on me right now, and smiling at me. Lord, please protect Ronnie's baby. Keep it safe from all harm. I promise God, that from this day forward, I will be eternally grateful for these blessings. Amen."

When I turned to go out of the chapel, I realized that the other person in the chapel was Michael. As our eyes met, I began to weep. He kneeled down and put his arms around me gently. I didn't resist. I needed someone to hold me and tell me that everything would be OK. He loosened his hold on me and I reached up and touched his tear soaked face. He understood what I meant even though no words were spoken between the two of us.

Dr. Carter came into my room and delivered the news that I, deep down in my heart, already knew.

"I'm sorry Ms. Spencer, but Ms. Foster didn't make it. She is still breathing, but only with the aide of a machine. She is clinically brain dead. She had a 'Do Not Resuscitate Order' in her medical records, however, due to the healthy baby she was carrying, we have not stopped life support yet. Do you wish to sign a waiver authorizing us to deliver the baby?

"I will sign any necessary papers you need me to sign Dr. Carter, just don't let anything happen to that baby," I said without even thinking.

My mind went back to losing my own child, and also to how bad Ronnie wanted to have a baby. There was no doubt in my mind about saving the baby.

"Very well then, we will go ahead and prepare for the cesarean section," he said.

"Dr. Carter, I would also wish to have Ronnie's organs donated."

"Most definitely! You don't know how many people are waiting on good healthy organs, Ms. Spencer, we'll get on that right away!"

I felt I made the right decision about donating Ronnie's organs. She would have wanted to help anyone she could. I just hate that I couldn't do the same with

Eric. He was injured too badly, and he was without oxygen for too long for his organs to be viable.

When the nurse came into my room, she brought Ronnie's personal items with her. Included in them was her driver's license. She was indeed an organ donor. After spending three weeks in the hospital, I was finally released to go home. When I drove up in front of the apartment complex, my heart stopped. Memories of the last time I was there flooded my mind. The last time I was here, Eric was here with me.

As I walked up the hallway, I could feel a gentle breeze pass over my body. It was as though I could feel Eric's presence around me. I opened the door to the apartment, looking in, expecting to see Eric's smiling face. It wasn't there. I walked into the apartment and sat down on the sofa. I could see the many pictures that we'd taken over the last couple of months. My eyes filled with tears. How could such a wonderful person be taken so soon?

When I walked into the bedroom, I noticed that the picture on the wall was leaning. When I went over to straighten it out, I noticed the safe behind it. That's when I remembered the last conversation that Ronnie and I shared and the gold envelope that she'd given me on the last day I saw here alive. She specifically told me to open it only if something happened to her.

I reached into the safe and pulled the envelope out and sat down on my bed. Moments went by before I finally got up enough courage to open it. There was a pastel pink piece of paper inside, along with some legal documents. Ronnie's favorite color was pink. As I looked a little closer, I noticed that it was a letter written in Ronnie's sloppy handwriting.

"Shaneeka, if anything happens to me, I want you to take care of my baby girl. Yeah, I know it's a girl because I had an ultrasound done. I wanted it to be a surprise. I named her Angel Shaneeka Foster. That's right Neeka, I named her after you because you are an Angel in my eyes. I wanted to let you know this because

some strange things have been going on. Ray has been threatening me, telling me that he's going to kill me and my baby! That's why I went to an attorney and had this Last Will and Testament drawn up that I enclosed with this letter. I wanted to make sure that if I wasn't around, my baby would be well taken care of. I know that you would treat her as if she were your own. I know that a lot has happened lately, and I hope that one day you can find it in your heart to forgive me for the pain that I have caused you. I never meant to do that. You are the only true friend I have ever had, and I don't ever want to lose that."

Love Always,
Ronnie

At first, I must admit I was kind of reluctant after all that had happened. When it came down to it, however, there was no doubt in my mind that I would honor her last wishes. Yeah, she made some foolish mistakes. We all have, but we'd forgiven each other and moved on. That's what a friend would do.

I immediately went over to the telephone and called the Department of Children and Social Services. The caseworker informed me that the baby had been placed in a foster home until other arrangements with family members could be made. I informed her about Ronnie's Will, and she told me to bring all of those papers down to her office first thing in the morning, and she would handle it personally.

Angel was such a beautiful little girl. She had many of her mother's features as well as her dad's. She was the perfect combination of her two parents. It was a bittersweet moment the first time I laid eyes on her. She looked up at me with those tiny little eyes and gave me an angelic smile. I smiled back at her, and pulled her close to me.

"Auntie Neeka is going to take good care of you, little one," I said to her and kissed her on her little cheek.

As I was sitting there watching Angel sleep, I looked down at my hand at my wedding rings. I slid them off my finger, and slid them onto the gold necklace that I was wearing. I wanted to keep Eric as close to my heart as possible.

I got up and went down to the storage room to take some of Eric's belongings when I came across my old jewelry box. I sat down on the floor and opened it up slowly. As I searched through the pieces of fake earrings and things, I noticed the ring made out of aluminum foil that Marcus had given me over eleven years ago. I smiled to myself, and remembered the words he uttered on the day he'd given it to me.

I ran across the room to another box and retrieved one of my childhood purses. In it, I found my "little black book". I still had Marcus's childhood telephone number. It still belonged to his mother. She gave me his new number.

As I waited for someone to pick up the ringing telephone, my heart skipped several beats. I was so nervous. I wondered what he was like after all of these years. He'd always been there when I needed someone to listen when I was a young child. With all that had happened, I needed someone to talk to now.

"Hello," the voice on the other end of the receiver said.

"Hi Marcus, do you have time to talk to an old friend?" I said.

"For you, Shaneeka, always".

Epilogue
One year later

Marcus and I still keep in contact with one another. He is happily married. I had a chance to meet his wife and two children. I wish him all the best. He is truly a dear friend. By the way, he is one of Michigan's most prominent and sought after Neurosurgeons.

Over the last three and a half years, Tyreek has been married twice, with no children. He calls me occasionally, but we both understand that a friendship is all that we could ever have. He is currently divorced.

Cedrick is still living the single life. I guess he is still making the ladies climb the walls. I see him occasionally, but we don't have very much to say to one another.

Xavier got married two years ago, and will become a father for the first time in a couple of months. He married a wonderful lady, and he is currently an associate minister at the church I attend. And by the way, he did forgive me for the way I treated him.

I was awarded full custody of Angel until Michael was discharged from the Rehab Center. Once he finished his therapy, he would take an active role in his daughter's life. Something that we both agreed would be best for little Angel. Although our relationship could never be the same, Michael and I remained close friends. Our new priority was to make sure that the baby had everything that she needed which included two loving parents.

As for Ray, he was convicted of first degree murder, and was sentenced to two consecutive life terms in prison without the possibility of parole for killing Ronnie in cold blood. He was also sentenced to twenty years for vehicular homicide because he caused the accident that claimed Eric's life.

As for me, I started going to therapy to deal with the loss of my loved ones. While in therapy, the molestation issues with Mr. Leroy came out. I now understand that none of what happened to me was my fault. I am no longer the victim, but a survivor. I made a report with the local authorities, and it was truly worth it. I had to go through, in detail, all of the nasty things that he made me do with him. He was picked up by the authorities. Once my story got out to the public, four other girls came forward and told of the things that he'd done to them as well. He was convicted on several counts of child molestation. Mr. Leroy was sentenced to life in prison. After serving only six months in jail, he died from a massive heart attack. He got off easy.

Will I ever find true love again? Only God knows for sure. I've taken the last year to rediscover who I am, and what I need to do in order to stay happy and healthy. Now, before I get into any other relationships, I will use this poem that I wrote to guide me. I hope you enjoy it.

If I gave myself to you

> Would you be there tomorrow
> If the skies weren't blue
> In times of darkness
> Sad, and lonely days too
> If my world
> Came tumbling down
> In the mist of troubles
> Would you still be around
> If I kept my body
> And didn't give it away
> Would you love me enough

Love Don't Live Here Anymore

To not go astray
I need to know
If your feelings are true
Would you be there tomorrow
If I gave myself to you

A poem by Angela S. Weathered

Angela Weathered

Printed in the United States
3949